No Quarter - Dominium
Volume 1

No Quarter - Dominium Volume 1

By MJL Evans and GM O'Connor

COPYRIGHT
NO QUARTER SERIES - DOMINIUM

Table of Contents

Acknowledgements

We would like to thank our sponsor who wishes to remain nameless and free from blame.

The Hurricane

August 14, 1689

Atia leaned over the railing on the forecastle of the *Aeolus*. She enjoyed being outside. The open air was invigorating. On the crowded main deck below, her mother, Lucretia sat holding Atia's three-year-old half-brother, while her sister Livia chatted to other passengers. So many people about to start fresh new lives; Atia envied them. They didn't have a price on their heads. They didn't have someone hunting them down at every turn.

She shuddered in the Caribbean sunshine. A creeping sensation traveled up her arms and along her neck. The last time she felt the cold was back on Barbados, when a rainstorm pelted the island for almost a week. Now *that* had been refreshing, unlike the past five weeks. Sharing passage in cramped quarters with over a hundred others was hardly ideal, but the journey was coming to an end. They were only hours away from Morant Bay.

From Morant Bay, Jonesy, a lifelong family friend, would smuggle them to Hope Bay, where Atia's father, Cormac O'Malley, planned to relocate them. Thanks to O'Malley's contacts in Port Royal and throughout the Caribbean, they had been transported from Barbados to Saint Lucia, where the *Aeolus* picked them up to make the long voyage. Atia hadn't seen Jonesy or her da for six years. *What did they look like now? Jonesy's hair probably went all silver, while Da's is white as chalk!*

A clergyman in a black cassock climbed the stairs and leaned on the rail beside her. She briefly caught his gaze. "Not long now," he said. "We'll be there by the morrow. Are you getting off in Morant Bay?"

"No, sir."

"You're Irish. How is it you made your way to Saint Lucia?"

"Sorry, sir. Me ma told me never to talk to clergy."

"Didn't mean to pry." The clergyman half-smiled. "Let's just be thankful the journey's at an end. The food here's rancid. It's been causing me Hell's own fury!" He turned to climb back down the stairs.

Atia giggled. *He's right about that, the food's bloody awful!* The wind picked up and the sun sank into the horizon. Atia collapsed her parasol. How she longed to see another sunrise in Hope Bay, a secluded fishing village on the north side of Jamaica beyond the Blue Mountains. She inhaled the salt air, imagining pink and orange hues seeping through the morning mist on the water.

Livia paused beside her sister. "What did he want then?"

Atia shrugged. "Who knows?"

Side by side, they were both beauties. At twenty, Livia towered over her sister by almost a foot. She had piercing pale blue eyes and deep chestnut hair. While seventeen-year-old Atia could pass as her mother's twin with flaming red hair and dazzling green eyes.

"Supper's soon," Livia said. "Are you gonna come down?" She gave her sister a doubtful look.

Atia grimaced. "I'll try." The passenger hold reminded her of the times she'd been locked in a closet by Hansel Crisp.

Livia squeezed her sister's arm before returning to the main deck.

A mantle of charcoal clouds stretched for miles across the sky and the wind rocked the small barque. Atia's body stiffened. A gust whipped the linen coif off the top of her head, unleashing a mass of curls. *Damn, another one gone!* The embroidered cap stitched by her ma spiraled into the dark mass forming behind the ship.

The supper bell sounded.

"That's seven," an officer called. "Supper's on, folks!"

Passengers filed down a narrow staircase to the hold.

The deep rumble of thunder echoed in the distance. The sea churned into an angry foaming beast. Atia gripped the wooden rail so hard it almost hurt. Her black boots tapped against the deck as Livia and her mother vanished down the stairwell. *I should be with them. I need to be with them.* She hated being afraid, but didn't know how to control it.

The officer on watch sounded an alarm bell, and the captainemerged from his cabin. "Take in the sheets! Get the passengers inside and secure the hatches!" He ran up the stairs to the quarterdeck to peer through his telescope at the fast-approaching Jamaican coastline.

Atia felt the first of the rain hit her face.

"I'm sorry sir; it just came up on us!" the officer exclaimed.

Atia shook. A tremendous crack vibrated the ship and the ocean sprayed her face. Her legs shuffled slowly towards the stairs, and then froze a few feet away. She wished Livia were there to wrestle her inside.

Atia remembered the times when she was regularly locked in the dark attic at Crisp's estate. Livia had loosened a ceiling board over the closet. With a candle to guide the way, Livia crawled on her hands and knees to bring her food and water. They'd pass the hours with stories and Celtic lullabies until Atia fell asleep.

Their secret ritual continued for weeks until one of Crisp's slaves turned Livia in. Cold dread consumed Atia when Crisp himself came to drag her sister from the attic. In the dining area of the slave quarters, he stripped Livia, hunched her over the table, and bound her hands and feet. Each slave took a turn at the whip. Atia screamed as she was forced to watch. Sometimes the sound of the whip haunted her dreams, intermixed with Livia's cries.

The cold broke Atia's train of thought. Tears flew off her face beneath a mighty gust of wind. She clutched the rail of the forecastle. Someone grabbed her arm.

"Atia," Livia said.

"Liv," Atia replied. "I can't go down there!"

"I know, Atia. But it's not safe up here. We must get below." Livia tried unsuccessfully to peel her sister's fingers off the rail.

The thought of the dimly-lit passenger quarters and people herded together in the shadows sickened Atia. The stale air reeked of perspiration, foul breath and worse. *I'd rather die than go down there!* She glanced over at the jostling crewmen securing the deck and climbing the ratlines.

Atia heard the yells of the captain shouting, "We're drifting to starboard. Turn her to port!"

"Shouldn't we stay on course for Morant Bay?" an officer argued.

The captain raised his telescope. "It's too late for that. We'll be thrown into Folly Bay sure as hell! We make for Port Royal."

Atia met her sister's eyes. "Leave me, go back inside!"

"Nay, I'm not leaving you!" Livia clung to the rail.

Damn it! Atia cursed herself. The water swelled, causing the ship to lurch upwards and crash down. Another vessel charged from the misty gray, flying a French flag with a gold fleur-de-lis at the stern. It came with such speed she thought they would collide. The men scrambled up into the ratlines and rigging to their stations while the vessel sailed north away from the rocks.

"Please, Atia, we must get below!" Livia insisted.

Atia took a few steps along the deck, and then froze, gripping the rail tightly. Nearby, stood the clergyman she'd spoken with earlier. Strange that he'd be outside in the storm?

An officer yelled at them all to get inside.

The clergyman gripped the rail of the forecastle. "To tell you the truth, I have a terrible fear of confined spaces."

Atia faced the growing waves; she had never seen a storm like this before. Her senses churned like the tide and panic burned through her, yet there was no place to run and no place to hide. The ship slammed back and forth while water soused the main deck.

"Atia! Livia!" came a muted voice on the wind.

Atia squinted to see her ma struggle against the gale trying to reach them. "Ma!"

Crewmen screamed. The mizzenmast snapped and toppled over. Flailing lines whipped through the air like blades, tearing a man in half. His bottom half dropped onto the deck while his top half flew over the railing. Red water pooled and the rigging collapsed, crushing several officers.

"Hold on; I'm coming!" Lucretia called.

Atia gripped the rail tightly. To her horror, a brutal upsurge clawed the deck, dragging Livia over the side. Shock paralyzed her for several seconds. "Liv!"

The clergyman swiftly reached down. "Grab my hand!" He caught hold and raised Livia up. Before reaching the deck, another swirling swell yanked them both over.

Lucretia patted Atia's arm and they both stared down into the foamy white.

"She's there!" Atia exclaimed.

Lucretia reached down to grab Livia and lifted her back up. Manic fear possessed Atia. No matter how badly she wanted to embrace her ma and sister, her arms remained locked around the rail. They were all clinging on for their lives now.

The ship collided against the rocks of Folly Bay. The hull shattered, releasing a loud groan, akin to a wounded animal in the throes of a death blow. Frantic passengers spilled onto the main deck from the hold. They climbed over and pushed one another, until they were finally tossed side to side and slammed over the edge of the ship.

Atia was pelted by flying debris. Her eyes briefly opened to behold a mountain of water as it rolled upon them. There was no air, only the rushing garble of the tide. Water relentlessly filled her ears and nose. Her lips recoiled into her mouth and her teeth clamped upon them. The water receded and she gasped, simultaneously sucking in air and spewing brine.

The rail began to buckle. Atia's eyes flickered open to a dizzying display of lightning. A short distance away, the rocks flickered and shined. Someone scrambled upon them. She recognized her ma's long hair. The ship's bow, only a few feet away, approached fast. With a potent hit, the front of the ship broke apart and her ma was crushed beneath it. Passengers flew mid-air, some landing in the water, others splitting apart on the rocks.

Atia opened her mouth to scream, but nothing came out. The rail broke loose and she was propelled forward, catching a ride along the spindrift to the stony beach. She landed heavily, her arms still gripped around the broken barrier. The scream finally escaped her throat and she belted it across the landscape. After unhooking her arms, she rose slowly, vomiting mouthfuls of salt water.

Behind her, the ship continued to splinter under the pounding waves. Flames erupted from the hatches of the hold. Unfortunate souls hurled themselves off the vessel to extinguish their clothes, only to be caught in the grinding undertow of the current.

The tide tugged at Atia's feet, toppling her backwards onto a rock bed. A hand grabbed her leg.

"I got you!" said Livia.

"Liv!" Atia clutched her sibling's arm frantically. Together they teetered to land. Another rush of water and curling waves towed them back into a sea littered with corpses. Arm and arm they fought towards the shore.

The water rose, driven by fierce wind. Atia was ripped away from her sister and stumbled over the surf. She reached out to grab at anything. Drenched in waves, her head was sucked under and she felt the brine plunge back into the ears, nose and throat. Momentarily she bobbed back up. Livia was only a few feet away.

Atia reached up and their hands locked. Together they hobbled madly for the beach, towing each other along. The instant the tide subsided they lunged onward to escape its grasp. Several feet away stood a jungle of trees.

Atia lagged for a moment, almost succumbing to the pelting wind and rain.

Livia tugged her arm and pushed her forward. "Move it, or we die."

At the treeline, they found a path. Grabbing at branches, they followed a seemingly endless maze of mud, vines, and roots. They reached a plateau surrounded by dense bushes.

Livia collapsed, rolling in next to the undergrowth for cover.

Atia could see down to the beach. The flames from the ship lit up like a beacon for miles through the murk. Carried on the wind were the screams of injured and dying passengers. They scrambled along the rocks only to be butchered by the waves.

Atia turned away, trapped between horror and extreme exhaustion. Through a break in the trees, she spotted the sails of the French ship caught in the hurricane. Grief consumed her and she lay down to embrace Livia waiting for the storm to pass.

Capitaine la Roche stood on the quarterdeck of his brig *La Lune,* and scrutinized the storm. He was no stranger to hurricanes and stared defiantly into the gloom. His vessel was rigged for merchant duty and they carried Cuban tobacco and ten tonnes of sugarloaf bound for Petit-Goâve.

The storm increased in its ferocity and water saturated the deck. The seasoned officers knew how to react, but he wondered how the new crew would respond to true danger. His thoughts turned to the English barque they had passed near the coastline. He tempered his sympathy knowing that death came fast to those who ventured near Folly Bay. La Roche lowered his telescope and turned to his quartermaster, François le Picard.

"North-northwest, Capitaine," le Picard said. He looked to the boatswain, Martel, and ordered him to check the barometer.

"Dropping fast. It *is* a hurricane. A genius he is, no?" Martel grinned.

Le Picard gave la Roche an irritated smirk. "You were right, Capitaine."

La Roche held out his hand.

"What? I'm good for it." Le Picard gave a sheepish look. "Besides, it is frowned upon at sea."

La Roche knew le Picard couldn't resist a wager. "Only when you're on account, you cheap bastard!" He watched the men hanging from sails, their bare feet clasping the ratlines. "Lifelines on deck, Monsieur Martel."

"Oui, Capitaine. Lifelines!" Martel ran to the main deck to ensure crewmen roped themselves to the shroud pinrail as the wind and rain whisked over the ship.

"Don't worry. A little rain, no problem!" la Roche assured as the sails flapped violently. "No, no! Take in the sheets!" He waved his fist at the men in the rigging. Fighting against the wind they struggled to tighten the lines. "Now make your course due north, Picard."

Le Picard turned to the young, muscular black man at the helm. "Monsieur Delacroix, twenty degrees to starboard. North we sail!"

Delacroix heaved the wheel. "Oui, starboard."

La Roche bobbed his head with a care-free smile. "Looks like it's going west. Just remain on course. Everything will be fine."

Le Picard cocked his eyebrow. "Going west, is it?"

La Roche shrugged. "Well, 'shit we are fucked' is not quite so uplifting! Yet we will try, Picard."

Rain pelted and waves slammed into the ship's hull.

Martel checked the compass. "Heading due north, Capitaine!"

Delacroix held the ship's course. *La Lune* pushed through the Jamaican Channel struggling against the disparaging winds.

Martel scanned the coastline through his telescope. "Ship, port side aft!"

La Roche and le Picard raised their telescopes. A flash from a lantern pierced the haze.

Martel squinted. "I think it's a fishing boat."

"A lugger," la Roche corrected.

The signal continued blinking.

"*La Lune de Miel*?" Martel said. "Looks like buccaneers, not fishermen."

"De Kreep." Le Picard sneered.

"That jerk buccaneer who is always sticking up for the Indians?" Delacroix asked.

"That's him!" le Picard snorted. "Probably on his way to attack Port Royal with a fishing boat and twenty guys!"

La Roche paused. His right hand trembled slightly and his throat tightened. De Kreep was as a brother to him and saved his life long ago. He shuddered, not from the weather, but the memory of a doomed raid that ended in the Darien Jungle in '68.

He would never forget the screams of his crewmates, the wet tearing of bloody flesh, and the scent of scorched human meat skewered over a blazing fire. His wrists burned from the rope. He sat within a circle of wooden pikes, next in line to be slaughtered. That's when de Kreep arrived with several Arawak elders. At first la Roche didn't understand why they were there, but soon his life was negotiated for and he was led away. To his shock and amazement, they reunited him with *La Lune*.

"Prepare to come about!" la Roche ordered.

Le Picard closed his eyes a moment in dread. When he opened them again, he gave an understanding nod. "Prepare to come about!"

La Lune turned hard to the port side, leaning dangerously, beaten by the gale. Crewmen clung desperately as they followed the flashing light. Officers fixed their telescopes ahead.

La Roche observed the men on the lugger bailing the boat out frantically. "Signal them. No grappling hooks."

"Oui." Le Picard took the signal lamp and flashed the message.

La Roche wiped the water from his eyes and squinted through the viewer. The buccaneers chopped down the rigging and the yard arms. The top sails fell and lastly the bowsprit was broken off the front of vessel and left to sink in the ocean. *Good man, Dashiell*, he thought, keeping his trembling hand in his pocket. *One shot at this – we must get them quickly, and then head to open water. Rocks are everywhere!* The wind and rain hammered the ship. He squinted at crew trying to furl the sails. "Beat them!"

The crewman struck the sails with their fists to purge the water.

Struggling against the elements, *La Lune* slowly fought her way to the lugger. The brig plunged into a large swell, and then propelled upwards, soaring into the air. Crewmen clung on for their lives. She slammed back down, causing an explosion of white water.

La Roche scrunched up his face. "That hurt!"

"This is going to get a lot worse. The storm, she is here. We should not be attempting this!" le Picard said. "Ready ropes and netting! Starboard side. Double quick!"

Martel and several crewmen prepared ropes, while others readied the nets. Men with axes stood alert. "Ready on main!" Martel signaled with a thumb up.

Le Picard turned to la Roche. "Main deck ready, Capitaine."

La Lune came alongside the lugger. The buccaneers leapt off and clung to the netting. De Kreep jumped last, just before the small vessel was sucked beneath the waves. When they reached the top, they hurled themselves over, landing on the deck.

"All aboard, Capitaine!" Martel shouted. "Cut the ropes! Throw it all over!"

"Turn due south for open water," la Roche ordered.

"Turn to port. We head south for open water," le Picard called, and then leaned to the Capitaine. "You know, having armed buccaneers climb aboard is not recommended even in nice weather."

De Kreep staggered up the stairs towards la Roche.

"Permission, Capitaine?"

They shook hands.

"I knew it was you. How do I ever thank you?"

"Even, this makes us." La Roche nodded, and then eyed Martel. "Get these men below, get them rested up."

"Oui, Capitaine!"

"Hold this course for as long as she can take it." La Roche addressed de Kreep, "Take your men below and take it easy. Then join in on the pumps. Martel will show you what to do. It's going to be a long fucking night, uh?"

De Kreep and his men followed Martel inside.

"Where will we put in, Capitaine?" le Picard asked.

"Let's survive the night first. Then if we have to, Port Royal."

Waves crashed over the deck.

"Nice knowing you!" le Picard grimaced.

La Roche relieved Delacroix at the wheel, tying himself to it with a pull knot. "If our time it is, *c'est la vie!*" He grappled with the helm. *La Lune* fell upon the back of another potent wave that drove the ship upwards and crashed back down. The sky lit up with brilliant slivers of lightning.

Rain pounded and howling gusts of wind blustered through the trees and bushes. Lightning cracked in the distance. Ma smiled and ran a brush through Atia's fiery red hair. The sun rose over Morant Bay. Ethereal beams of light broke through the mist. Da smoked fish wrapped in tobacco leaves over a small fire. Her stomach grumbled.

Atia's eyes opened sluggishly. The cold damp ground made her body ache. "Ma?" she cried hoarsely and sat up. The hanging sleeves of her dress had been torn away. Atia massaged the cuts on her exposed arms. Her left arm had been branded with an iron cross by Crisp. In retaliation, her ma had ankh symbols tattooed on their arms to cover the scars.

Atia rose to her feet, kneading her bruised ribs. The stern sat half submerged on the beach below. Corpses and wood fragments scattered everywhere. Behind her a field of sugar cane and patches of jungle lay in ruins.

"Ma?" Atia called softly.

Her sister moaned and rubbed her eyes. "Atia?"

"Where's Ma?"

Livia rolled onto her side. "She's in Elysium. No more harm can befall her."

Atia turned to face the sugar field. Wherever home was, it had been swallowed by the storm. *If I had just reached out my hand to grab her, she might be here with us now.*

Livia whimpered, trying to stand. "Bloody hell!" She vomited salt water, doubling over in pain. "Can't…breathe."

"I'll find clean water." Atia hoped rainwater was trapped within the cane. Lifting long broken leaves, she managed to suck back small mouthfuls. When she had her fill she brought over a few stalks for Livia.

Atia braced her ribs with one arm and knelt beside her sister, trickling water down her throat. She cradled Livia's head and gently brushed hair away from the gash on the side of her face. From behind them footsteps sloshed through the wet mud. A voice said, "I hears something!"

The splashing and rustling drew nearer. A group of emaciated slaves in torn rags emerged with their ankles bound in shackles. A short, portly white man covered in dirt pushed his way through, whip in hand.

"What is it? Who's there?" He grinned through yellow teeth

and rubbed his hands together. "Well, lookie here, tasty little morsels. And who might you be, me lovelies?"

Atia trembled. "Please help us, sir? We've been put through the mill."

"Irish as four-leaf clovers too," he jeered. "Immigrants? Indentured pikeys?"

"We was on a ship," Atia explained. "It broke up."

"Ah, the shipwreck. You could fetch five hundred pounds apiece! Who needs crops when ya got pikeys, eh? Bring 'em to the ship!" he shouted at his slaves and then kicked at their chains.

The slaves grabbed at Livia, who screeched with pain.

Atia pushed them. "Get away from her!"

The slaver struck her across the face. Atia recoiled, touching her split bloody lip. She reached for her sister's arm.

A slave pointed at Livia. "This one's hurt."

"Of course she is, ya imbecile!" the slaver bellowed. "Bring 'em! She only need live long enough for sale." He yanked the chains and the slaves hauled Atia away. She tried to fight them off. The slaves lifted Livia as carefully as they could and the girls were transported through the field down towards a small dock, where a weathered lugger sat. Upon its missing nameplate at the stern, a mossy stain formed the name *Sweet Dreams*.

"Ready to make sail!" the slaver hollered to the workers aboard, who were in the midst of repairs. "We're going to Port Royal!" He pointed at the slaves before heading towards his house. "Put them in the hold!"

Atia stumbled along to the dock. A short distance along the beach sat a village with a dozen storm beaten cottages and a stable. Fishing boats sat tied up at a wharf. *We could escape on one of those boats!* Atia glanced back to the house, where the slaver entered the front door.

One of the slaves stopped. "No one is watching. Go now, run!"

Atia was released and she rushed to Livia's side and tried to lift her.

Livia writhed in agony. "Go on Atia! Leave me!"

Atia tried to lift her sister again. "No! I'll not leave you."

"Save yourself, Atia!" Livia insisted.

She wouldn't leave her sister. They always watched over and protected one another. They survived the worst kinds of trouble because they stayed together. One such instance was back on Barbados when they carried out their cleaning duties on Crisp's boat-house. After removing weeds and overgrown vines from outside, they swept the interior and polished the windows.

Crisp arrived to criticize and hassle them. Atia was grabbed by the hair and tossed to the floor. It gave him great pleasure to remind her that she was breeding stock as he raised her skirt and spread her legs. She didn't hesitate for a second and clawed his face with her nails.

Livia joined in with a boat-hook off the wall and lunged at Crisp. She managed to gash the side of his head. He fell, clutching at the wound. Livia grabbed Atia's hand and they ran for the door. Their retaliation was short lived however when they came face to face with Crisp's slaver captain who stood over seven feet tall and wore barbs on his knuckles. Atia and Livia were soon locked up to await punishment.

Atia knelt on the dock beside Livia. "We go together or not at all."

One slave motioned to the others and they lifted Livia down the beach towards the village.

The dirt covered slaver emerged from the house with a bottle in his hand and two ruffians at his side. "Ya ungrateful savages!" His thugs seized the chains. The slaver approached Atia, uncorking the bottle and pouring in the contents of a vial. "Just don't know when to quit, do ya?" He revealed his yellow teeth and forced the bitter liquid down her throat. "We're all going to Port Royal now."

Atia Crisp

Port Royal

Capitaine la Roche gazed through the window of his cabin aboard *La Lune*. The morning sunshine cast an orange glow on the English city of Port Royal. It was a miracle they made it with the sails in tatters and wreckage spread all over the deck. He fell in and out of consciousness fused to the helm all night. Only when he saw blue sky with seabirds floating overhead had he realized that they survived. He remembered Martel releasing the rope and de Kreep helping him to his cabin. After suffering a headache and waves of nausea, la Roche woke hours later, almost recovered.

His bluish gray eyes studied the many fishing boats and Turtle Crawls, where the city's turtle supply was farmed in two large pens. Four years it had been since he set foot here and everything appeared the same. He however was now in his forties, his dark hair marred by silver streaks and he bore many more scars.

He finished buttoning his shirt to conceal purple bruises on his torso from being pinned against the wheel. After slipping on a respectable dark blue jacket and black trousers, the finishing touch upon his head was a black wide-brimmed hat. The leather belt around his waist held a cutlass and a Spanish stiletto. It would only be a matter of time before people realized he was back. Known by many names, he was Gator Gar and El Capitaine when he raided the Spanish, le Sage to the buccaneers of Hispaniola, and La Salle when he was sent to England with Henry Morgan to be tried for piracy. He managed to keep his true identity secret; after all diligence was paramount, enemies were everywhere.

The interior of the cabin was simply furnished with a writing desk, chair, corner-bed and a royal blue banner on the wall with gold fleur-de-lis and a faded family crest, given to him by a friend on Cayman Brac Island. Christened Jean-Paul la Roche, he never knew his family. They had been killed long ago. He grew up in a workhouse and escaped before the age of ten, and later served aboard a galiot named *Rascal*.

A knock sounded. "Oui," he summoned and le Picard and Delacroix entered.

Le Picard seemed refreshed and wore a simple black suit with gold buttons, and black leather bucket boots. He removed his felt hat decorated with an ostrich feather. François le Picard served as quartermaster and sailing master. In his late thirties, he was the youngest of three brothers. His eldest sibling Pierre was a privateer, with the reputation of a fierce pirate. François had tried his hand at pirating, which had failed miserably, resulting in many deaths.

Delacroix wore his usual leather vest and cut-off trousers. Being young and ambitious, Delacroix fell into disappointment when his only task was to help transport sugar. Even so, la Roche had the look of an experienced pirate, with elaborate tattoos on his arms. He gave the impression that there was more to him than being a simple merchantman.

"Crew's making repairs, Capitaine," le Picard said, glancing down at the gold longsword on the desk. "The sword? Someone's getting promoted or killed."

La Roche smiled scathingly. "How did you make out?"

"The Harbormaster will let us stay for two days. They're unloading supplies for us at the end of the north dock."

"Take whatever they lay down but clear away when she's loaded and find a spot in the harbor out of the way." La Roche admired the weapon glistening with rubies and emeralds. "It's time I gave you both more responsibility. I'm taking shore leave. Broke my balls, this trip did. Command is yours for a couple of days, Picard. Congratulations."

"Thank you, Capitaine, but if I had a hundred men and fifty pounds of coca leaf powder I couldn't do it in time." Le Picard strapped on the belt housing the longsword.

"Then your new master's mate will help you." La Roche watched Delacroix's face light up.

"Me?"

La Roche nodded. "I'm promoting you. Congratulations. Find some place out of the way. Work fast, but do it right. Remember, hostilities are growing. We could find ourselves in an enemy port at any moment. Keep on your toes. Get to work on the mainmast first."

"Oui, Capitaine!" Delacroix rushed excitedly from the cabin.

"See? Enthusiasm and youth will see us through."

"Enthusiasm and youth? Are you jesting?" Le Picard shook his head.

"I know you preferred Martel, but I've known him a long time. He's a good man but he's not meant to lead. He walks with his head down sometimes and even crashes into people."

"Oui, he does," le Picard agreed. "I know. But Delacroix? Fucking, that's all that kid knows. I for one don't want a bunch of women swimming after the boat!"

"He'll be fine. Stop your bitching." La Roche laughed and they walked from the cabin up the stairs to the main deck.

"Being back here, someone will recognize you."

"Don't worry. Nothing will happen." La Roche held out his arm and a large dark gray parrot mounted his shoulder. "A quick drink at the Swiftsure, things will be fine." He befriended the bird many years ago and trained him to carry messages. La Roche always make sure there was a supply of dead insects around to keep Minuit motivated.

Le Picard's face sagged. "Attracting too much attention you are and the Swiftsure Tavern of all places!"

"No one is going to recognize me, trust me." La Roche rubbed his chin. "I'm yesterday's news." He took a dead cockroach from his pocket and Minuit snapped it up. "Ok. Go stretch your wings." The parrot took to the air, soaring over a mixture of new and old buildings.

Arrow approached the harbor – a thirty-gun frigate with a walnut-colored hull and red and gold trim. White sails with mauve border fluttered in the breeze. The ship listed to starboard. Captain Arthur Valentine, a former privateer and now the top shipper of Port Royal, better known as Bleedin Art, stood on deck like a scarecrow inspecting the harvest. Art picked at his large teeth with a silver toothpick. Not only did he have a head for business, he loved the arts, particularly writing poetry. Art even had the audacity to write a letter to the late Earl of Rochester, telling him he was an over-indulgent drudge who wouldn't know true poetry if it gave him syphilis. Later, a reply came with two simple letters on parchment – F.U.

"Gun cay due east, Captain," his first mate Ginger noted the landmark indicating the route to Port Royal. "Ready for the turn."

Art peered through his telescope. Gusts of smoke rose over the city. Hundreds of ships congregated in the harbor. "They ain't here. I can see every bloody mast all the way to Ligania and they ain't bloody here." His was a sinewy English accent. He retracted the viewer. "And where the bloody hell is the pilot boat?"

"She may be sunk. Looks like Port Royal got a piece of it herself."

Cupid, a red Cuban Macaw, circled the vessel, landing on Art's shoulder. Art grinned painfully. "Why did I buy those caravels?"

"I said those ships were too old."

"Did I blame you?" Art stared at the sea. "Bloody hell!"

"Bloody hell!" the macaw agreed.

Ginger tilted his head. "You can always blame Rook."

Art nodded. "Aye, I can blame him. Ya just wanna see Coggshall cut his balls off, you ruthless prick! Nay, it's me own damn fault this time. The investors are gonna be pissed."

"Ruthless prick!" Cupid screeched.

Ginger pointed across the water. "*Diamond Dog*. She's sailing in ahead."

Diamond Dog was a pretty two mast Shnyava with grayish blue sails, and an oak-stained hull patterned with diamonds. Being a light reconnaissance vessel, it was similar to a brig, but much smaller. It reminded Art of his days as a young privateer aboard the *Falmouth* in '59.

Royal Rook, known also as Lieutenant Marquess Castle, was recently hired by Art for added protection and for his previous experience as a privateer who once served the city. Rook's mission was to escort Art and the slave ships to Port Royal. At this point however, the storm may have swallowed the lot.

Art pounded his fist on the rail. "Oh, Jesus Christ, we lost it all!" How he longed for the good old days of simple pirating and pillaging! He despised the slave trade. His wife's family made their fortune in it, thus the only reason for his involvement. *If I could only commandeer a Spanish treasure ship and have a wild drunken spell in Tortuga, I'd be a new man!*

Cupid landed on the taffrail next to a swivel gun. "Bugger it!"

"You shut it! I don't need any of your beak!" Art aimed his pistol and the macaw took off, shitting on the deck as it went. He took a deep breath and thought of his favorite writer, Shakespeare. "Shoulda stayed out the picaroon racket, bugger it!

True is it that we have seen better days. You know the way, Ginger, take us in." He snarled at Port Royal. "There's four months down the bloody hatch!"

Diamond Dog made her turn at Fort Walker, sailing into the inner harbor and around Fort James, heading to the King's Wharf to dock. Royal Rook peered through his spyglass. *Ah, bloody hell, no sign of them caravels!* He lowered the viewer and rubbed the back of his neck. His fingers glided along a diamond-shaped tattoo on the left side of his throat, the result of a drunken, rowdy excursion to a pirate haven known as the Blarney Stone on Cayman Brac Island.

His quartermaster, a wide hulking man named Tiny McAllister, stood at his side. A former crewman of the *Falmouth* under Bleedin Art, Tiny met Rook during a pirate raid. "Any sign of them?"

"Nay," Rook spoke with a stodgy accent.

"Shall we dock?"

"Aye, take us in." Rook whistled. A brown and gray Mascarene parrot named Checkmate circled above.

"I preferred piracy to this lot, mate," Tiny said.

"Aye." Rook screwed up his face. "What the bloody hell did I get us inta this time?"

The ship coasted alongside a sizable wooden dock, where other vessels assembled to be inspected by the Harbormaster. Rook, Tiny, and eight crewmen jumped off to secure the *Diamond Dog* with rope. Checkmate swooped down, landing on Rook's shoulder. Waiting for them on the dock stood two of Bleedin Art's cutthroats.

Rook hated dealings with thugs. Things had a tendency to go awry. He took a deep breath and faced Pikestaff, a typical pirate with a patch over his left eye, simple clothes, and a blue and yellow Martinique Macaw named Gibbet. Beside him was Jag'd Jayne, a run-of-the-mill thug, early twenties, broad shouldered, and dressed in plain black trousers with long boots and a brimmed hat.

Gibbet eyed Checkmate, initiating a staring competition.

"Mr. Coggshall would like to know why yer here and the merchandise ain't?" asked Pikestaff.

Rook gritted his teeth. "We lost them."

"I warned him. Stay away from wanna-be privateers." Jayne smirked.

"You lost them all?" Pikestaff folded his arms.

"Art packed the whole lot inta two old caravels." Rook removed his hat and ran his fingers through his hair. "Wasn't my call, mate."

"Not yer call? Be sure to tell Mr. Coggshall that when he cuts off your balls."

"I was hired by Bleedin Art and it be his own damn fault they went down. When he arrives I be expecting payment."

"Aye, be sure to tell him that when he gets here." Pikestaff lit his pipe. "Art may lose a ball or two himself!"

"*Arrow* coming in, sir," *Diamond Dog's* lookout called, pointing to the ship rounding Fort James.

"Better duck, Lieutenant, it be aiming for you," Jayne said.

"Oi, clear the docks, you lot. Official business only!" The stern voice came from Harbormaster Jonathan Pepys, a graying man with a clay pipe poking out of this mouth.

"Say hello to your little songbird for me," Jayne added before walking off with Pikestaff.

Katie Evans. Rook flushed a bit as he thought of the girl he hadn't seen in ages. A pang of guilt tightened his chest. He had left when Coggshall took over the slave industry. Rook despised both equally and didn't want to work with either. He promised to return and take Katie away. *Whether I'm paid or not, I'm taking her away this time.*

Further along the inner harbor at the dock of Waterman's Wharf, another ship landed, a sloop named *Bloody Mary*. A true beauty, with dark red sails and a rosewood-finished hull. Captain Alfonse Slazerelli named her after Mary Rose, a whore he mutilated in Belize. She'd been a work of art that Mary. He slit her throat and watched the blood drain. Next, he severed her limbs and strung up her entrails on copper wall sconces. Captain Slazerelli licked his lips and lit up a pipe before stepping down the gangway. He'd earned the name Slasher Al – the demented, the twisted. *The artistic genius.* He grinned to himself.

He'd seen *Diamond Dog* and *Arrow* come in and decided it was high time to apply for Bleedin Art's position. Al disembarked, wearing his red dress suit and black leather vest that concealed a dozen sharp knives. They whispered to him softly, craving blood. "There, there, me beauties. Soon, very soon." He patted the vest like a truly impulsive madman.

He sashayed towards the Crooked Compass. Upon his shoulder sat Lash, a female macaw of Dominican green and yellow, her wings clipped. His loyal thugs followed. Big Fred was six and a half feet tall, and his talents included crushing heads with his fists and eating live reptiles. Then there was Dogfish, who filed his teeth down to sharp points and reveled in biting the flesh of his enemies. Good men, good cutthroats, not afraid to get their hands dirty.

Al followed a quaint stone path to the tavern. Slave trader Heins Burghill stood on the terrace staring into Cherry Red's Boutique at the erotic activities inside. He sucked on a fat Cuban cigar and drank heavily, until his cheeks turned a festering red. The sound of broken glass snapped him from his daydream and he marched inside.

Al stepped through the entrance and meandered towards a table near the window, avoiding glass fragments. Big Fred and Dogfish followed, grabbing a table on the terrace.

"Clean it up, idiot!" Burghill yelled, throwing an empty bottle at one of the male slaves.

Al sat down.

Burghill glanced over briefly, grabbing a fresh drink before he took the seat opposite Al.

"Fatima!" Burghill yelled. "Fan!"

"Yes, Mr. Burghill." The beautiful young African girl fetched a large bamboo fan and initiated a steady breeze.

"What can I do for you, Captain Slazerelli?" Burghill grimaced.

"I believe ale is in order."

"Ale!" Burghill barked, signaling to a slave.

"Word hath made its way that you have lost them both, Mr. Burghill."

"What do you mean, lost? Who says?"

"My sources say *Arrow* and *Diamond Dog* left Barbados with two caravels and five hundred of your property." Al paused, staring at Fatima. *Gagged and bound with rope – she'd be perfect!* "Them ships be in the harbor but there be no caravels."

Burghill chewed on his cigar. "He lost them?"

"I can't help but ponder the idea that had I been trusted with this venture, things may have turned out favorably for all involved." Al puffed his pipe, and then grabbed the mug of ale off a tray from the slave. He took several large gulps and gawked at Fatima again.

Burghill stood up and paced, patting his greasy forehead with a silk handkerchief. "So we have hundreds of buyers and we got no new slaves or whores. He bought caravels? That cheap ass son of whore! This is a disaster!" He collapsed into his chair.

Al sneered at Burghill's distress, but really couldn't blame him. Caravels were an outdated design that ignored the influences of wind change in favor of social hierarchy. Upper class passengers would stay in the elevated cabins at the bow and stern of the ship, while the lower classes stayed below, all the while sailing nowhere fast.

"I'll have to tell Coggshall. We need every piece of shit slave and whore we can scrounge up." He glowered at Al. "Don't touch Cherry's girls. Not yet."

"I was promised two harlots meself from our previous venture and I intend on collecting."

"Well, it's gonna cost you more 'cause ya never return them! We can only hope Coggshall has some…"

"Fresh meat?" Al grinned maniacally and Lash released a loud shriek. His eyes darted to Fatima. "I'll give ya two hundred pounds for her."

Burghill's face crumpled up. "She mends wounds and speaks eight different languages. She's worth ten times that!"

"A bit expensive for me taste. But perhaps as a signing incentive."

"Play yer cards right and anything's possible." Burghill puffed on his cigar and peered out at the water.

Fort James guarded the entrance to the inner harbor. Cannons lined three sides. On the top level, next to the flagpole, Acting Lieutenant Governor Dorcas Dewar strolled along with a silver walking stick, dressed in a lavish purple suit, feathered hat, and heavily polished buckle shoes. His companion Chief Judge Lord Lawrence Llewellyn was decked out in a finely woven long coat and feather trimmed tri-cornered hat. They walked around the slaves cleaning up storm debris.

Following them was the Governor's advisor, Mason

Sleemans, dressed in a dark doublet and matching trousers with a tri-cornered hat.

"Splendid idea, Larry! Splendid!" Dewar clasped his hands together.

"Seems the appropriate thing to do after a hurricane."

Sleemans's eyebrows pointed up. "Pretend to give a bloody damn?"

"Oh, you're so right. For spirit at the very least. That's politics for you, it's all about the people." Dewar shook his head. "Bloody sods!"

"My thoughts exactly, sir." Llewellyn shook his pen, a newfangled invention nick-named the 'Pepys' pen, inspired by Samuel Pepys, cousin to the Harbormaster. "Why won't this work?" He tried to write on parchment.

"You turn it. The ink's inside," Sleemans explained

"Supplies may be short, so we may have to dip into the reserves just a bit." Dewar lifted his thumb and forefinger.

"Of course, sir. No problem. The audit is my responsibility, after all." Sleemans bowed, exhaustion permanently etched on his face.

Dewar paused. "A hurricane is a disaster and that's what the disaster fund is for, right? We'll call it the I Survived the Hurricane Ball."

Llewellyn clapped childishly. "Excellent choice, your Grace!"

Dewar breathed deeply. "I love when you call me that."

Sleemans glared at Llewellyn. "Shall we impose a curfew for the lower classes?"

"Absolutely!" Dewar clapped his hands together. "We don't want the riffraff spoiling our fun." He watched a pair of city officials emerge from the top of the stairs. "Here comes the I Want, I Want Brigade!" The city's engineer, Bill Chitty, and Councilman White charged forth. "Councilmen, what is it?"

"Ya wanted the damage report, sir," Chitty replied.

"Ah, of course. Let's have it."

"Thames Street to High Street from the King's House to the Admiralty Court is flooded," White said, clad in a white suit, with a white wig and an ivory walking stick. "My house as well. I'm thinking of renting out the basement as a bath house."

"The bridge to the Palisadoes is out again," Chitty added. "We'll need to appropriate funds from the disaster bank for a new bridge – a proper bridge."

Dewar shook his head. "I'm afraid that's impossible, funds have already been appropriated."

"What?" White demanded. "I haven't seen anything about that. You better not be planning another ball at our expense!"

Sleemans interjected, "If I may, gentlemen. There's currently not enough in the disaster fund to cover a new bridge. However, I suggest a sufficient amount be withdrawn to cover the cost of a temporary replacement."

"Which will disintegrate in the next hurricane." Chitty folded his arms.

"But for now, it will have to do."

"Where will we make up the difference?" White queried.

"Well, you're the council chair." Dewar gave an encouraging smile. "Sit on it for a while. You have until next season."

"We also have extensive damage to the streets. Cracks and fissures have opened up," Chitty said.

"Well, why aren't the streets paved?" Dewar played with handle of his walking stick.

"They can't be paved; they are filled in each time they're damaged. The ground's too soft to get a solid foundation without major excavation."

"Use some kind of interlocking stone," Sleemans suggested.

"This is unacceptable! We're English, damn it! We know how to build things where they shouldn't be!" Dewar bellowed.

"I suggest taxes be raised on the lower classes to cover it," Llewellyn said. "We'll call it Chitty's Infrastructure Tax."

"Perhaps I can think of a more suitable name," Sleemans reproved.

Harbormaster Pepys approached the gathering.

"Very well. Fix the bridge, Chitty, and no lollygagging," Dewar directed.

"Ah, Pepys!" Llewellyn began. "This is an ingenious invention!" He held up the metal pen. "How does it work?"

Pepys turned it and scribbled against the parchment.

"Ah, there it is! Marvelous!" Llewellyn snatched the pen back. "Thank your cousin for me."

"You're welcome. If you need it refilled take it to Pope's Tobacco on Honey Lane."

"Splendid!"

"Pepys, I noticed a lot of foreign ships in the harbor today." Dewar cleared his throat.

Chitty and White took the cue to leave.

"Two Spanish pinks and a French brig. They each entered under a white flag and subjected themselves to inspection. They all be civilian ships with extensive damage and wounded. We couldn't refuse them," Pepys explained.

Dewar tilted his head. "Of course not, that wouldn't be very Christian. We'll charge them a fee."

"I think a large fee would be appropriate," Llewellyn said.

"Quite right. Have them each pay, uh ..." Dewar trailed off, confused by all the currencies being phased out in favor of the new monetary system. "Do they still use doubloons these days?"

"I believe so."

"Have them each pay four gold doubloons."

Pepys frowned. "Four doubloons?"

"You think it should be more?" Dewar did not want Port Royal's hospitality to be taken advantage of. "Well, let's say—"

"Four will be fine, sir."

"Oh, hurrah!" Dewar's sight stopped on a ship with decimated pale yellow sails near Turtle Crawls. "What ship is that over there?"

"*La Lune*, sir. A French brig loaded with sugar. I've given her two days to make repairs."

"Well, he looks like he can afford it." Dewar mused. "You can start with that Frenchie. Get your men on it right away."

"Aye, sir." Pepys departed.

"Commanding, sir, very commanding. If I may say so."

"Oh, you may. It's up to us to make the important decisions, Larry." Dewar's eyes widened. "It should be a costume party!"

"Dress as your favorite natural disaster?" Llewellyn's eyebrows perked up.

"What a good idea. See to it immediately, Lord Llewellyn!"

"Right away, sir!" He gave an exaggerated salute that imitated the mating dance of a bird of paradise.

Slasher Al

After the Rain Comes Good Weather

Admiral Christian Goddam cursed under his breath. Atop the tower at Fort Charles, he stared through his telescope at the dozens of wounded ships gliding into the harbor. In its thirty-year existence, the city had seen its share of war and suffered frequent attacks from the Spanish and Dutch. Now under threat from their former ally, the French, the five forts lay waiting to see action again. "My God, look at them all! We should let them all drown!" Goddam huffed. The threat was imminent now. His adversary across the chess board was none other than the famous Dutch privateer, Laurens de Graaf. Not only a military genius and working for the French, Laurens had successfully sacked Vera Cruz in the last great pirate raid of '83.

Lieutenant Lance Thorne stood beside him. He spat into the harbor.

"We're outnumbered ten to one and that idiot Dewar thinks we're perfectly safe! I feel like Priam watching the Greeks arrive at Troy!" Goddam barked. *I know they think I'm a fear monger, but the city could be taken at any time!* Under the current government, the city's defenses had been sorely neglected. The five forts were manned on a voluntary basis, leaving the cannons plagued with dirt and overgrown weeds. Also, he only had two ships at his disposal for the defense of the city: *Falcon*, a sloop with a dozen guns, and *Drake*, a small frigate with eighteen guns.

"What's your count, Lieutenant?"

"Four more French, one Spanish," Thorne said. "Most of them are merchant vessels and can hardly float."

"Don't be fooled. This is the kind of opportunity Laurens waits for. You never know when the enemy will strike!" Goddam glanced up just in time to see an ugly dark bird fly overhead and shit on him. "See? That's what I mean! Caught off guard, we're sitting ducks out here!" He used a handkerchief to wipe it off, but instead made the mess worse.

"It is said to be good luck, that." Thorne pointed.

"Aye! The best of luck, Thorne, thank you!" Goddam growled. "Shoot that bird!"

Thorne raised his pistol and shrugged, indicating that it was empty.

"Move *Drake* and *Falcon* to the middle of the harbor and remain at battle stations."

"Aye, sir." Thorne saluted.

"I want every militiaman on double duty, and cancel all leave. We're on the brink and no French Trojan horse is penetrating this man's defenses, not while I'm alive!" Goddam clenched his fist and sneered at the vulgar dark bird as it glided over the fish market.

Throughout the Turtle Crawls market and along Fisher's Row, merchants unloaded barrels and crates. The oily pungence of fresh fish wafted from the merchant stands. Scaly delicacies included snapper, mackerel, tuna, marlin, and grouper. Seabirds skulked around and stray cats wandered among the wooden planks and between crates seeking scraps.

La Roche and de Kreep paused at a stand for a quick meal of smoked tuna skewers and boiled shrimp. They washed it down with a pint of ale from the Three Crownes Tavern and continued to walk until they reached the top of Lime Street.

De Kreep had changed out of his storm-beaten clothes into a brown leather vest and dark trousers. He wore a long musket on his back, his cutlass and dagger on a leather belt. Messy dark hair gave him a youthful appearance despite the fact that he was in his thirties. With a mixture of Arawak and African roots and a sprinkling of French, he had developed an exotic reputation among the brothels for his tribal tattoos and piercings. He used the alias de Kreep to protect his true identity, Dashiell Dupris. "*Après la pluie, le beau temps.*" He marveled as everyone picked up the pieces and carried on. "I leave you here, Capitaine. I'm going to go find a whore."

La Roche shrugged, lighting a pre-rolled cigarette. "When in Rome."

"Find a whore!" Minuit squawked, stalking them overhead.

"They are called strumpets here," la Roche said.

"Strumpets here! Strumpets here!" Minuit screeched.

La Roche tossed a dead beetle in the air. The parrot caught it, and perched upon a wooden post above a torn sign indicating NO…UMPING. "The good ones are on Thames Street, yes?"

"Well, I can afford Lime Street, no," said de Kreep.

They shook hands.

"Give the gang my best."

"I owe you a debt of gratitude, Capitaine."

"Even, this makes us." La Roche turned down an alley leading to Lime Street. Within seconds de Kreep vanished. Like a truly experienced buccaneer he knew every pathway, secret shortcut, and available escape route.

La Roche cringed at the thought of sticking it anywhere near Lime Street. He ambled along the lane, lost in thought. A young blonde woman in a low-cut dress approached him. "If yer lookin' for company sir, I be exactly what you be needing." She smiled, and flopped out a breast.

He tipped his hat and walked by. Granted, he hadn't had a woman in a good long while. He had an incurable penchant for redheads that stemmed from his youthful liaisons with the fiery Jacquotte Delahaye. They lived happily enough until their differing views caused them nothing but misery. She took off with a group of pirates to start The Freebooter Republic near Santa Catalina. La Roche cut across to New Street, where a skinny prostitute with dirty hair accosted him. "How about a bob for a bob, mate?" She grinned with missing teeth. He raised his eyebrows. *Enter at own risk, huh?*

A wherryman trundled by, and la Roche jumped onto the back of the carriage.

The vehicle turned up High Street and halted at the great brick wall of Fort Rupert. La Roche leapt off and paid the driver. He crossed a makeshift bridge to the Palisadoes – a little village with a cemetery near the water's edge.

Although compelled to pay his respects to his fallen comrades, he felt very alone wandering around headstones. La Roche and the Brethren of the Coast had a falling-out long ago. He had been implicated in the disappearance of Roc Braziliano and two thirds of the loot from a Panama raid. Since then, only two other Brethren members remained alive. *This is what it's like to be almost extinct.*

At the foot of a monument, he knelt down and cleared away wildflowers, branches, and storm debris. And there it was, a skull and crossbones with the words:

Barbadosed
Here Lyeth ye Body ye Sir Henry
Morgan, 1635-1688

It was the first opportunity he'd had since his banishment to pay his respects. La Roche removed a bottle of rum from his jacket, uncapped it, drank deep, and poured the remaining contents on the grave. "Drink well tonight, *mon camarade*. Say hello to the boys, Ed, Diego, Davy, and Jamie."

Minuit perched upon the grave stone and said, "*mon ami*."

La Roche smiled appreciatively and tossed him another dead insect.

The parrot snapped it up. His overly large beak seemed to smile back. Then his dark wings spread and he was off, soaring back towards Fort Rupert.

Minuit glided all the way down High Street over the Meat and Produce Market. He landed near the aptly named Bird's Alley across from the Merchant Exchange, a triangular layout of numerous buildings stacked side by side. All the major merchants in Port Royal assembled with over a hundred shops joined together by pathways and staircases. One could easily get lost for hours within ladies' apparel, men's shoes, pastries, books, jewelry, children's toys, pipes, tobacco, and the Wine and Spirits Shoppe which offered liquor from Italy, France, Africa, and London.

From the northwest corner of the exchange, Dr. Sander Strangewayes strolled towards Sea Lane. He wore a burgundy long coat and black breeches, his brown leather medical bag in hand. As he passed the bakery, the aroma of imported apples and cinnamon swirled through the air. He inhaled deeply through his crooked nose and continued across the lane where he approached his assistant, Miles Gladstone, a stocky man with brown skin.

The doctor had adopted ten-year-old Miles on a trip to Barbados, and brought him up in the apothecary trade. Miles grew to know basic chemistry, healing arts, and was critical in running the doctor's business. More than thirty years later, Gladstone remained a faithful assistant and trustworthy friend.

"Oi, why are you dropping that here?" Gladstone asked, watching slaves pile wood debris.

"It's all being moved to the top of Thames Street, sir."

"What for?"

"Bonfire fodder for the Governor's ball."

"Not another one. He burned down the orphanage last time!"

Gladstone smirked, and then turned to the doctor. "Thames Street is all cracked up and flooded. They shouldn't bother to fix it and just call it Canal Street."

"Quite right. Any news?"

Gladstone scratched the back of his head. "I'm afraid so. A Frenchie reported a barque going down off Folly Bay. Fishermen say there's bodies all over the place. Women and children."

"Any word of survivors?"

"In Folly Bay…?"

Almost a year ago the doctor was contacted by an old friend, Cormac O'Malley, who needed help to smuggle his family away from the slave trader Hansel Crisp. O'Malley knew the doctor's true business of smuggling slaves with a perfect success rate. His business was so cleverly clandestine that none suspected he was anything other than a concerned doctor and the town's Chief Surgeon.

Strangewayes's concern grew. "We should head out there."

"But the fayre?" Gladstone reminded. "It's tomorrow night."

"Oh shit, I almost forgot."

"The girls are counting on ya. How about I head out to Folly Bay and find out if it was them? It's better you stay here and let me take care of this one."

Strangewayes patted him on the back. *Ah, good old reliable Gladstone!* "Then you must head out there straight away. Let me know as soon as you find out."

Gladstone paused. "What if it really was the *Aeolus*?"

"Then I'll be giving the O'Malley's some bad news."

La Lune

Giving a Bloody Damn

At the corner of High and Lime Street stood a Tudor-style building with a steeply pitched roof and chimney. It was a quaint design with timber framing, brickwork, and diamond-shaped windowpanes with lead casings. Waiting outside the main door stood silver-haired Mrs. Abigail Beazley.

Strangewayes climbed the steps to let her in, realizing what day it was. "Good day, Mrs. Beazley."

"Good day, Doctor." She smiled. "Is now a good time?"

"Yes. Let's get started, shall we?"

The doctor put the closed sign out in the window. They marched upstairs to the study, where stacks of disorganized papers buried the desk.

"Good Lord, I have my work cut out for me!" Mrs. Beazley sat down to skim the insurmountable stack. After an hour of collectively flipping through information, the weary doctor retreated to a window seat. *I'll never get used to this new money system!* He sighed and glimpsed down at the busy street below. Pedestrians and carriages shifted along, while strumpets and beggars persisted in their trade. Behind him, Mrs. Beazley prattled on regarding his bookkeeping and finances.

"Yes, Mrs. Beazley, I understand." He leaned his head against his arm with all the enthusiasm of a student being scolded by his teacher.

"If you don't stop robbing Peter to pay Paul, you're going to go broke. It's that simple!" She shook a piece of paper at him. "So much for keeping inventory. You keep giving things away like you're the only doctor who—"

"Gives a bloody damn?" Strangewayes tilted his head.

She lifted an empty vial off the table. "You gave away the last of the laudanum? Or shall I chalk this one up to personal use?"

The doctor flushed. "Another fisherman lost an eye. I had to give him something. Besides, I didn't know a hurricane was coming. Hurricane prediction is not listed on the sign."

"But you need to sell it to them. You're not going to survive in the new-money world if you keep giving things away. When the tax collector comes you'll have nothing to show for it. They will clean you out."

"Yes, well, that's what I have you for, isn't it? To help me survive in this money world. You worry about what it says on paper and I'll worry about where it comes from. I didn't vote for this pestilent system, so why should I have to bloody live in it?"

Twenty-four years ago, the doctor had been forcibly relocated to the Caribbean so that his radically advanced and non-Christian views would no longer burden England. "I have a new batch of laudanum in the supply room, capped this morning." His eyes strayed down to a carriage halted in the alley beside the apothecary. A woman in black emerged, and his heart palpitated. "Goodness me, this is a first!" He slipped on his best longcoat with a hibiscus flower pinned to the pocket and patted down his hair. "I'm sorry, Mrs. Beazley. As much as I value your sage advice, we'll have to pick this up later."

"A paying customer I hope and not a debt collector?" Mrs. Beazley gave him a critical glance as she held up a piece of parchment and a 'Pepys' pen.

"Don't worry. I'm on a winning streak." He paused to sign the paper before descending the staircase.

The storefront bell rang for a second time. The doctor opened the door to Esmeralda Belford. She was a blond beauty with the most enchanting hazel eyes. For the longest time he thought he was in love with her. Long ago, when he was a ship's surgeon, he'd sailed with Rowdy Belford, her late husband. He witnessed firsthand her strength and kindness. Gossip among the pirates earned her the nickname Easy, which fueled many daydreams. Today was the first time she came calling outside shop hours.

"Doctor, I'm glad you're here."

"What can I do for you, Mrs. Belford?" He beamed, admiring her curls.

"I'm afraid you're needed at the Smith's Alley landing," she said. "That horrible little Magott has slaves in the hold of his ship. They appear to be sick and Sheriff Tellam won't let them out."

"Damn! Didn't Coggshall ban him from selling slaves?"

"Evidently not."

"One moment, I just need to gather a few things." Strangewayes grabbed his large brown medical bag, stuffing it with extra supplies.

"And they call me Widow Bell now, Doctor, haven't you heard?"

"Yes, I know." He followed her outside.

"We'll take my carr," she said, leading him to the white and gold horse-drawn carriage. "When I go deaf they'll be calling me Dumb Bell." She pursed her lips into a faint smile.

Strangewayes smiled too, climbing aboard with her.

"Sorry to kidnap you like this, Doctor, but these people look like they're dying." She released the brake.

"No, not at all. Thank you for alerting me." Their eyes met for moment before she snapped the reins and the carriage took off. They wheeled down Queen Street, past King's Ground. After making a left down Smith's Alley they pulled up near the common area by the water, where a small lugger christened *Sweet Dreams* was anchored.

Strangewayes could already hear arguing between Sheriff Tellam and Johan Magott.

"For the last time, no! I'm going to have to confiscate your ship and cargo until it's been inspected by a doctor."

"Nobody's confiscating nothing! They be special delivery for Mr. Coggshall."

The doctor helped Widow Bell down and they advanced.

Tellam shook his head. "Fine, then we'll ask Coggshall when he gets here!"

"He's paying five hundred pounds each for the whities."

"What whities?"

"Two of them, girls."

Tellam leaned over the hold. "What's he want with them?"

"I hears he was paying big fer pikeys." Magott shrugged. "As fer the Indians, I figured I'd sell them. Me crops are gone anyway."

Strangewayes's eyes widened. *White girls? Pikeys? I must look in the hold! Perhaps O'Malley's family survived after all?* As he and Widow Bell drew closer, a carriage arrived, tailed by a wagon that pulled up right next to the docked ship.

Councilman Bernard Coggshall in his finest clothes was the first to step down, his hair covered by a felt hat. Burghill followed, dressed in a mint green ensemble with matching woolen cap. From the wagon emerged Coggshall's newly hired cutthroats – Slasher Al, Big Fred, and Dogfish.

Tellam tipped his hat. "Mr. Coggshall, sir."

Coggshall knit his brow, noticing Widow Bell.

She charged forth in a huff. "Coggshall, you disease-infested carrion, yer behind this!"

The cutthroats roared with laughter and Strangewayes tried to restrain her.

"You again?" Coggshall sickened of her thorn in his side.

"This don't concern you, Mrs. Belford," Tellam said.

"The hell it don't. Magott is banned from selling slaves in Port Royal. You agreed to it yerself, Coggshall!"

Coggshall peered into the cargo hold. He came straight away when word reached him that Magott seized pikeys. It had been many years since he'd seen Crisp's property, but the hair of the two girls, flaming red on one, deep chestnut on the other, was unmistakable. Coggshall practically trembled; he was certain it was Atia and Livia Crisp. The day finally arrived and now Crisp's balls were in a vice! He'd use the girls as a bartering chip or cash in on the price on their heads. *Soon I'll be the wealthiest slaver in America!*

Strangewayes approached the hold. "Disgraceful! As Chief Surgeon of Port Royal, I am responsible for the health and safety of the public; I therefore confiscate these people in the interest of public health!"

"Mr. Coggshall has final say in this matter," Tellam said.

Coggshall tried to contain a smile.

"We've been over this. This boat breaks several recently passed laws. For heaven's sake, I can smell the feces!" The doctor's nostrils directed him to Magott. "Unless that's you?"

"You ain't taking me slaves. I got a God-given right to sell slaves. If Mr. Coggshall don't want them, then they goes up fer bids."

"Well your God-given boat invites something we in the science community refer to as disease. Please, Sheriff. All of these people need to be in my care right away."

Tellam covered his nose with a handkerchief. "Do something with them; they're stinking up the harbor! And get those poor girls out of there!"

"Bring them up!" Magott called.

"Them Indians aren't fit for sale," said Coggshall. "But I'll take them girls though!"

The door to the hold swung open. Atia and Livia were dragged out by Magott's thugs. Both women slipped in and out of consciousness, sick, drugged, covered in mud and filth.

"See their clothes!" Widow Bell gasped. "They're not slaves!"

"They must be shipwreck survivors!" Strangewayes insisted.

"That's right, shipwreck survivors. I finds them and that gives me salvage rights!"

"Salvage rights don't apply to girls, you product of inbreeding and rotgut!" the doctor yelled.

Atia came to for a few moments. "Where's Ma, Livia?"

The sweet sound of victory! Coggshall rubbed his hands together. "Strangewayes can have the Indians. I claim ownership of the girls."

"These girls aren't slaves if they're shipwreck survivors!" Widow Bell argued.

"Crisp of Barbados reported a missing family of Irish indentured servants bearing his name. They escaped his custody," Burghill explained. "Mr. Coggshall's got a lien on all Crisp's property due to an outstanding debt." He handed a document to Tellam. "A Letter of Recovery signed by Lord Spotswood entitling Mr. Coggshall to seize any property belonging to Crisp."

Tellam inspected the document. "The redhead said 'Livia.' There's a Livia Crisp on the list."

"That doesn't prove anything!" Strangewayes protested. "Sheriff, at the very least, for your own safety and the safety of the people of the city, I beg you."

"It's settled, Doctor," Tellam said.

"What's settled?" Widow Bell was exasperated. "No it isn't!"

"Absolutely not! These people are under quarantine and under my charge," the doctor argued.

"Mr. Coggshall has proof of ownership!" Burghill said.

"This isn't over!" Widow Bell said. "I demand a hearing be convened!"

"A hearing on what?"

"A hearing to determine if you can still be considered a man when you have such a small prick!" She flipped up her middle finger.

Slasher Al and his men sniggered.

"Mind yer tongue, woman, or I'll cut it out!" Burghill took the dagger from his belt.

"Like you did to little Katie?"

"You mean Mute Katie?" Burghill snorted.

"You cowardly troll, these are human beings! Unlike your kind, the sludge of the gutter!"

"She needs a lashing, Mr. Dogfish." Coggshall grinned; it was truly a great day.

Al's thug removed a whip from his belt and struck Widow Bell across the arm and face. She fell into the doctor's arms.

"Oh, that be unfortunate." Coggshall shook his head. "Best be off with ya before we have another … accident. Do we understand each other?" He eyed Al. "The lady needs attention. Escort her and the Doctor to the Apo-thery. We'll have the slaves sent on presently."

At blade point, Strangewayes and Widow Bell were hastened into the carriage. The horse snorted and the vehicle took off with the doctor at the reins.

"What ya want done with them?" Al asked.

"For now take the carr. Keep them pinned down at his place. Let them know who's boss." Coggshall put a fat cigar in his mouth. "You can have her later."

Al flashed a frenzied grin. "Aye."

"This one's just yer type." Coggshall pointed to the red-haired girl. "Too bad she's spoken for."

"There's the matter of me signing incentive."

"Just be there tonight and you never know."

Al climbed into Coggshall's carriage. "Oi!" He signaled Dogfish and Big Fred. Soon they were on their way to the apothecary.

Coggshall turned to Burghill. "Have Valentine's surgeon inspect the Crisp girls. But, first things first, join us for a drink at the old ship, Sheriff?"

Tellam tipped his hat. "I'd be delighted."

"What did you want done with the Indians?" Magott asked.

"Give them a lethal dose and drop them off at the Apo-thery as promised and go get cleaned up. You can afford it now. I have a room for ya at the Swiftsure." Coggshall entered Tellam's carriage.

Widow Bell held a handkerchief to the side of her bleeding face. It wasn't the first time her views landed her in trouble. She'd been sent to Bridewell Prison once for being part of an anti-slavery group. Pardoned by Governor Dewar himself, whose exact words were, "your husband was a Port Royal hero and you have nice tits, oh, hurrah for tits!"

The carriage pulled up alongside the apothecary and Strangewayes jumped down hurriedly.

"Think I'll continue home if you don't mind, Doctor."

"I think it best you come inside, quickly now!" He reached for her hand.

Slasher Al charged into view.

"Shit! They did follow us! Dog sodding bastards! What do they want?"

Widow Bell climbed down and Strangewayes ushered her inside, where he double-bolted the door.

"Let me see."

"I'm fine." She held her face.

"Of course you are. Come with me." He guided her to the parlor.

Mrs. Beazley joined them with a tray of medical supplies and a bottle of rum. "By the looks of it, I'd say a drink is in order?"

Widow Bell laughed. "Please."

"Thank you for your expert commentary. Now, we need to prepare for patients," he replied sharply, dipping some cotton in alcohol. "And there are unfriendlies outside, so please stay in and keep the doors locked."

"Good day to you, Mrs. Belford." Mrs. Beazley retreated to the examination room.

"And to you, Mrs. Beazley."

Strangewayes knelt beside Widow Bell and gently brushed her hair behind her ear. "I don't believe I've had the pleasure of your company in my establishment before."

"There must be something we can do." She gazed into his striking blue eyes. "I can't believe we're sitting here while those poor people are detained."

"This isn't over. I promise you." He dabbed her wound.

"A lot of good we're doing from in here." She flinched.

"I'm sorry. I was a little outnumbered."

"That's not what I mean. I have nothing against you, Doctor. On the contrary, my husband and I always respected you. I know you sailed with him, though he never spoke of it."

Widow Bell came to Port Royal at fourteen with her parents, Peter and Annabelle Bartaboa. Her father was a famed carpenter who built the gallows outside the Marshallsea Prison. One day her mother and she stopped in at the Swiftsure Tavern to pick up a couple crates of apple cider. When they tried to leave pirates accosted them. Slasher Al and Roc Braziliano were among them.

"Let me help ya with that?" Al leered.

"No, thank you," Annabelle said.

Another pirate blocked their path and Rowdy Belford stepped in. "What's the problem?"

The bartender pointed. "These two are hands off by order of Mansvelt. She's the town carpenter's wife, she is."

"He don't tell us what to do. Fuck the Dutchman!" another pirate yelled.

Al grinned. "You can if ya must, but I'd rather fuck these little tarts meself."

Braziliano stepped in as brawling began. "Come now, we're all gentlemen here. My men act like degenerates sometimes ladies. Come have a drink with me. Let me make amends."

"Nay, sir. We're needed at home," Annabelle argued.

Braziliano never took kindly to being a refused a drink with any woman. "Now that ain't friendly. A drink is all we was askin' for."

"The ladies said no and they be under protection of the Dutchman," one of the French pirates opposed.

Braziliano reached for his sword and unsheathed his blade. "Ya dare to talk back to me, lousy toad!" His cutlass swung through the air cutting off the pirate's head and slashing Annabelle's throat.

Widow Bell would never forget the expression of complete shock on her mother's face. The crates of cider dropped and the glass bottles shattered on the floor. Blood spurted from the gaping cut. She clasped at her mother's throat, trying to stop the bleeding, but blood jetting through her fingers. Soon the lifeless body of Annabelle dropped to the ground.

Possessed by grief and anger, Widow Bell grabbed one the broken bottles and lunged for Braziliano. She managed to slice the side of his face before being punched down. That's when Rowdy and his men stepped in with raised swords.

Widow Bell gazed at the painting of the brig, *La Lune de Miel*, sailing into the north dock with Fort Walker behind it. A dark gray parrot stood guard on a post. "I know that ship. Which one did you sail with, l'Olonnais or the Capitaine?"

"Both." Strangewayes smiled reservedly. "Shall I prepare a bandage?"

"No need, Doctor. At this point in my life I couldn't give a shit about a couple of scars." She rose and glanced out the window to see Slasher Al. *Bastard!* She frowned. He noticed her straight away and made obscene gestures with his forked tongue, grabbing at his groin.

Strangewayes clasped her hand. "No, please don't go outside just yet. It isn't safe."

"You're right about that." Her hand entwined with his. "I've treated you coldly over the years, haven't I, Doctor?"

"Not at all. You've always been very polite."

"To tell ya the truth, I never knew if you were so nice because you genuinely care, or if you just wanted to get into me goods." She gave him a coy stare.

"Perhaps a little of both." The doctor's eyes gleamed. He flushed, and then began to manically tidy the counter. "Where has that Mrs. Beazley gone?"

"Coming, Doctor," she called, entering with a tray of tea and biscuits. "Sorry, I should have left something for you to clean." The women glanced at one another.

"I miss the pirates," Widow Bell professed. "Not the current lot of scallywags, but rather the old crowd."

"I know who you mean." Strangewayes peered out the window into the golden orange sky. "And yes, we could certainly use their help right now."

"If I only had the means to eradicate them all, believe me, I would."

"Indeed," the doctor agreed. "That would be ideal."

Esmerelda Belford/Widow Bell

Man of War

A battered man in a black cassock limped down High Street. To the casual observer he was either very drunk or had been beaten senseless, tossed down a flight of stairs, and then smashed over the head with a barrel. Whoever he really was, he had been known by several names including Ballock and Dirk. Currently he was titled Skean. Agonizingly, he dragged himself through the square of Admiralty Court and hammered on the door. His arrival was met with no response and timing was critical. A light flickered from the window upstairs.

He huffed in a lungful of air, preparing for the climb up by unstrapping the leather case from his shoulder and removing its contents. Contrary to appearances it contained only a scroll. With a broken arm he latched onto the stone crevice and willed himself up, hoping that by the end of the ordeal he'd be rewarded with a brandy and a chaser of laudanum. He grunted, reaching the outside of the chamber.

Inside, he could see Admiral Goddam preparing to call it a day, downing a glass of booze and removing his jacket. Goddam unbuckled his sword belt, setting the rapier on a table. In the reflection of the mirror, Skean knew he'd been spotted. Unintentionally he crashed through the frail glass of the window and slumped onto the floor. He stretched out his hand to deliver the scroll.

"Good God!" Goddam knelt beside him. "Take it easy, son." He examined the scroll, popped open the red seal and scanned its contents which declared:

> Orders to the Admiralty, new government to preside
> over Port Royal. Military units are to stand down.
> Place local authorities under house arrest:
> Lieutenant Governor Dewar and Lord Llewellyn.

The Admiral's eyes bulged. "Oh, bloody hell!" He leapt up and pulled a bell cord until a knock came at the door. Lieutenant Thorne marched in, saluting.

"Send word to the forts immediately to stand down!" Goddam ordered.

"Sorry sir? Stand down?"

"Aye, that's the order! Get it out to all the forts double quick! I don't want any of the lookouts to raise the alarm. Tell them all to stand down!"

Skean breathed a sigh of relief. With his orders delivered, his mission was now complete. His eyes rolled into the back of his head, and he passed out.

Major Thomas Paine neared the harbor on his galiot, *Rascal*. A small swift ship with furled sails, it was the size of a wasp compared with the vessel it towed, *Relentless*. The colossal Man of War overshadowed everything in its path. Over one hundred and eighty feet long, armed with seventy-eight guns, it was the size of a small city with multiple levels and ornate carvings painted red and gold. The figurehead was that of a golden lion holding the English coat of arms.

Paine glanced back at his charge, awestruck to be in its presence. In his fifties, he had over three decades of service to the Crown as a privateer and dozens of pirate raids under his belt, having served with Henry Morgan, Gator Gar and Roc Braziliano. He dressed simply in faded black with a deep scar burrowed into his left eyebrow. "Detach," he ordered, aiming his telescope at the city. "Let her run."

Crewmen axed the ropes that towed *Relentless* and the galiot raised its oars. *Rascal* glided into the fish docks of Turtle Crawls, letting the larger ship drift to the short arm of the north dock.

Paine jumped from the ship's edge carrying a blunderbuss, a wide-barrel shot gun capable of inflicting devastation at short range. He held the barrel with his three-fingered left hand and glimpsed around suspiciously. All was clear. He turned his head in surprise, recognizing *La Lune* off the long arm of the north dock. *That's the last ship I expected to see in Port Royal!* Signaling *Rascal's* captain, half a dozen crewmen leapt off to secure the galiot.

Two men disembarked. Judge Harold Goblet, no more than four and a half feet tall, terribly stout with a round head and big lips that gave the impression that he was always pouting. Beside him stood a man with a chalky white complexion, white hair, and pink eyes. Goblet removed a bag of coins from beneath his judicial robe and handed it over. "For your services, Major Paine."

"Secure Fort Carlisle and await orders," Paine instructed, stuffing the payment into his jacket.

"Aye, sir." The captain saluted. The crewmen jumped back aboard, while the oarsmen pushed the ship off.

Paine escorted the judge towards the north dock, while the pale man took off into the night. His first task was complete.

Across the water at the long arm of the north dock, *La Lune's* crew loaded supplies. Le Picard and Martel stood in the rigging to observe repairs to the mainmast, while Delacroix managed the deck hands carrying sail cloth. Le Picard was disappointed they couldn't find it in yellow.

Delacroix looked across the water and his mouth dropped. The massive warship silently approached in the darkness. "*C'est pas vrai!* Oh … Capitaine?"

"Oui, what is it?" Le Picard turned to look and almost fell backwards. "Look at the time! All hands prepare for departure!"

"*Merde!*" Delacroix trembled.

Le Picard and Martel swiftly climbed down. Once on the main deck they went downstairs to get their jackets and weapons.

"Oh, I'm yesterday's news, he said … nothing can go wrong, he said!" Le Picard scowled, securing his sword belts before tearing back upstairs. "Get her ready to sail. We are going to get the Capitaine. Wait here," he ordered Delacroix.

"For how long?"

"Until we get back!" le Picard snapped and pushed Martel along. "Come on, we must get to the Swiftsure." They ran down the gangway.

Upon the short arm of the north dock a crowd gathered beside *Relentless*. Pepys the Harbormaster, Major Paine, and many others stood in awe.

Le Picard and Martel slowed, trying to slip by unnoticed.

"Blow me down! That's a Man o'War!" a dock hand said.

"Blimey, it is!" another gasped. "What's she doing here?"

"You mean *he*," said another.

"Rather hard to miss that," Pepys said. A pipe hung from his mouth and wafts of smoke billowed around his head.

"She is here to transition a new Lieutenant Governor by order of King William." Paine removed a scroll from his jacket. "I hereby commandeer the harbor and these docks by order of Lord

Spotswood of the Leeward Islands. Clear the area and order that ship away." He glanced at *La Lune* and addressed the dock hands. "And she's a ship; the captain is the Man of War."

"Aye, sir, right away," Pepys agreed.

Le Picard and Martel almost cleared the crowd. Martel tripped over his quartermaster and ended up with an elbow in the gut.

"We must not be seen!" le Picard whispered.

They escaped the area and entered the city, racing towards the Swiftsure Tavern.

Relentless crept forward, a silent monstrous beast. Her captain, a titan of a man, perfectly matched to her ferocity. Known to pirates as Big Dick, Captain Richard Longstaff was six feet tall with broad shoulders and dressed in a royal blue jacket detailed with gold stripes and black buttons. His sight set on Port Royal, and he gestured to his first officer, James Fishhook, who manipulated a signaling mirror to contact the vessel *Incorrigible*.

"*Incorrigible* is in position, sir. The harbor entrance is secure."

Standing on the bridge, Longstaff inspected the city, his eyes on Major Paine, and the cigar he held remained unlit.

Unlit. The city is not secure. "It looks quiet," Longstaff said. The last time he had been here was after the battle of Roatán in '85 where he served under Paine. It had been a blood-soaked skirmish that all but wiped out the buccaneers. Longstaff was hired by Paine to escort the Whigs to their new official duties in Port Royal.

Longstaff felt the eyes of the King William's Whigs. They loitered behind him. He bore nothing but the utmost disdain for their arrogance, lack of battle experience and their ridiculous powdered wigs. "The city is not secured."

"Why is it unsecured?" Acting Lieutenant Governor Peter Piper frowned beneath a vast silver-blue wig. Beside him stood Magistrate Harry Mold, who wore an equally large adornment in a dark brown. "Where are Admiral Goddam's men?"

"The man on the inside must not have completed his mission," Mold speculated.

Longstaff retracted his lens. "Or, he may not have arrived at all. Captain Bentley?"

A man in a blood-red waistcoat stepped forth. "Aye, sir?"

"Ready your men. We're going ashore on time."

"Aye sir, we're ready." Bentley saluted.

"Very well." Longstaff turned to the Whigs. "Gentlemen, it hasn't gone as smoothly as I'd hoped. Seems I will have to go ashore after all. If you'd care to wait on board?"

"If it's all the same, Captain, I still have confidence in your plan. We're going ashore," Piper said.

"Aye, your Lordship." Longstaff nodded. "Stand behind us at all times; there may be pirates in the city."

The gangway lowered from *Relentless* onto the north dock. Scores of Red Royals, special marine soldiers, disembarked to form a perimeter led by Longstaff and Bentley. Piper and Mold followed to meet with city officials who arrived by carriage.

"Admiral." Longstaff saluted.

Goddam shook his hand. "Dick."

"Admiral Goddam, what kept you?" Piper asked.

"We only just received word tonight, your Lordship."

"Have the forts been ordered to stand down?" Mold pressed.

"The forts are all secured, sir."

Judge Goblet approached with the mayor.

"Giblet, where is your wig?" Piper glowered at the short man's partially bald head.

"Goblet, sir. It's being powdered, it gets so sticky here."

"You'll wear your wig and you'll wear it with pride! Do I make myself perfectly clear?"

"You do, sir. I beg your pardon." Goblet's bottom lip threatened to quiver. "Captain Longstaff, may I trouble you for a handful of men to accompany me to the courthouse?"

"Captain Bentley, see to it."

Bentley saluted and ordered his lieutenant to the task.

The mayor stepped forward, dressed in a tailored suit of deep green and a pleated waist coat of black velvet. He held a walking stick with a silver lion perched on the handle. "Welcome to Port Royal, your lordship."

Piper stuck his nose in the air and gestured to Mold. "You may address Magistrate Mold with matters of government until my staff comes ashore."

"Wake all councilmen. There will be an emergency session this morning to proclaim the new government," Mold ordered.

"Yes, sir," the mayor replied, "but most live on plantations."

"They're all ex-pirates and they're all here. Wake them!"

"Captain Bentley, move your group into the city. We're going to secure the King's Ground as a temporary headquarters," Longstaff instructed.

"Aye, sir." Bentley and his men marched to the causeway.

Longstaff turned to Fishhook. "Jim, take your men and secure the King's warehouses."

"Aye-aye, sir."

"Very good. We should press on," Piper insisted, pushing past the officials on the way to the carriage.

Major Thomas Paine

Lonely at the Top

The Black Dog Inn, although rough at times, had its charms. The interior walls were nicely appointed with black walnut panels and you'd never see a finer collection of Elizabethan oak wainscot chairs with pin wheel carvings. Upon its floor lay a red carpet accented by a blue arabesque border.

Dr. Marcus MacAskill finished his sixth round of whiskey and was now acceptably drunk. He came to Port Royal in '55 on the *Torrington*, the same ship that brought Bleedin Art. They became instant friends and worked together ever since. Meeting Nadele happened ten years later. His eyes lingered on the table near the fireplace where he'd proposed. She died giving birth to his son, who also perished. From the start, there had been trouble. It had been too late in Nadele's life for her to have children, but she had been just as stubborn as he. After that he couldn't bring himself to attend births ever again.

That's when MacAskill developed his reputation for being a rabid reptile and an ill-tempered Scot who should be deported. Now, in his early sixties, his gray hair was long and wildly out of control. Traditionally he wore a faded black coat with matching breeches, weathered long boots and a gold band on his finger to commemorate his wife.

"Right, let's move out!" MacAskill ordered the newly hired lackeys he drank with.

One was Mace Scarcliff, in his early twenties; he wore basic cotton trousers, a vest, and a brimmed hat. The other two hires looked the part of greasy thugs; unkempt with clothes so tattered, not even the poorhouse would have them. Ironclad and Stutters climbed onto the driver's seat of the doctor's red coach with two large black wheels at the back and two smaller ones at the front. Twin horses snorted at the crowd.

Pedestrians swarmed in the direction of the north dock.

"Now what the bleeding hell is going on?" MacAskill snarled at the commotion. Huge masts over-shadowed the rooftops and a new English flag flew at the stern. "It's King William's forces! Holy Father's rain o'shit, it's a Man o'War!" He jumped into the back seat. "Get us to the captain's house now!"

Stutters honked the horn. "G … g … get…"

"Get out of the way!" Ironclad finished.

Charity week, is it? MacAskill looked at Scarcliff. "He's hired lepers too, no doubt?"

The carriage sped up High Street to Valentine Mansion.

Bleedin Art sat on a large couch propped up by plush cushions, bathing in heat from the roaring fireplace. The Inferno Room was his own private sanctuary and the only place where the ache in his rheumatic knees would let up. He took a long drink of rum and gazed nostalgically at the ornate carvings of ships and sea battles on the wall. *Can one desire too much of a good thing?* He enjoyed the company of Burghill's European strumpets.

"Oh yeah, that's it, right there!" Art exclaimed. A woman's head bobbed up and down in front of him. Natalia was a pearl. Young, voluptuous, brunette, and adorned in the finest German fabrics. Her cleavage bounced up and down as she massaged his knees. Catharina, on the other hand, was tall and regal with porcelain skin. Her light blonde curls strayed over her shoulders, a crown to the extravagant Românian gown she wore. Her fingers firmly pressed on his neck, washing away the tension.

Art's precious few minutes in Elysium were snuffed by a knock at the door. He patted Catharina's arm. "Get that, would ya, love?" She opened the door to MacAskill. "I wanted one bloody night to meself! What's so bloody important?"

"King William's Forces are here!" MacAskill grimaced. "They've taken the city."

Art exposed his huge teeth. "Right bloody now?" He signaled the strumpets to move away and set the rum bottle on the table.

"Aye, right bloody now. A Man o' War has taken the north dock. What the bloody hell are we gonna do?"

"Jesus Christ on a fiery knipple!" Art unrolled his pant legs and stood up. He strained his knees putting on his long boots and turned to the lovely ladies. "You girls make yourselves scarce." Limping over to the coat on the door, he grabbed a coin bag. "Here, take a couple of days off."

"Mr. Burghill will be cross." Natalia stuffed the bag into her bodice.

"You don't worry about it. I'll talk with him. You two just stay home." He escorted them to the door. "And stay away from

Slasher Al; I mean it! You don't wanna know him." Art gulped back some more rum before calling, "Stinger, get in here!" A secret passage opened beside the fireplace and a thug emerged. "The timing's bad, is all. They'll be calling for Dewar's arrest."

"Better him than us," Scarcliff said.

"It all ties back to us. He knows too much." MacAskill folded his arms. "We'll have to kill him."

Art's eyes widened. "Kill Dewar?"

"Kill Dewar!" Cupid the parrot squawked from a perch in the corner.

"Aye. Send Pikestaff, tell him it's on Coggshall's order."

"He wouldn't buy it. And besides, it's too late to *do* Dewar. But Coggshall, on the other hand, they'll think he was done by his own cutthroats. We'll never get a better chance." Art pointed at Scarcliff. "You and your men, get over to the Swiftsure. Kill Coggshall before the Whigs get to him."

"Coggshall's kid, too?"

"All of them, damn it! Then go to the Crooked Compass and do Burghill. Call it a structural reorganization. Oh, and have me wife sent to the beach house in Ligania."

"Ru ... ru ... ru..." Stutters replied.

Art eyed MacAskill. "What the bleeding hell's wrong with him?"

"Maybe you should have asked him when you hired him?"

"Right, we'll take care of it," Ironclad finished.

Art scrutinized their shabby clothes. "Get yerselves cleaned up and presentable for the new government. Get the pirates out of the city before all hell breaks loose and keep it orderly! All of ya get a move on!" Art slipped on his dress coat and tidied up in the mirror beside the door. He shrugged, disenchanted.

The thugs dispersed and soon the doctor and Art were alone in the Inferno Room. Both of them lit up cigars. "Gets lonely at the top, does it?" MacAskill puffed.

"You know it." Art gulped back the rest of the rum.

At the King's House, a celebration was in full swing. Costumes ranged from simple masks and cloaks to storm debris strapped to one's body. The night's musical entertainment was the local group Trinity, comprised of a fiddler, guitarist and flautist. Giant kegs filled with signature ale from the Swiftsure Tavern sat beside tables lavished in food. Savory sausages wrapped in pastry, miniature meat pies, smoked snapper, cheeses, and imported fruits lay on silver trays.

Governor Dewar practically stomped his feet when called away to the study to attend some outstanding business. He sat tapping his feet against the side of an enormous mahogany writing desk, reviewing documents. Slaves fanned him with large feathers while Sleemans handed him another parchment. "Fine, this is the last one. Then I'm getting back to the party!"

"Or, you could just leave the seal with me and I could sign them all for you."

Dewar eyeballed him suspiciously.

"This is to appoint Mr. Binge as postmaster," Sleemans explained.

"But, he's black, isn't he?"

"Technically, five-eighths black, sir."

Dewar's face contorted. "Oh, no, no, no. That simply won't do. He's at least three shades too dark for public office."

"Not according to your current amendment."

"I told you, damn it, we need a color chart! What happened to Mr. Brooks?"

Sleemans sighed. "You had him killed, remember?"

"I did?" The governor cocked his head to one side.

"Yes. He was arrested for dumping shit out a window onto the street and executed. You made dumping shit in public streets a Capital offense."

Dewar nodded. "We had him arrested, of course. That's filthy. What are we, French? But I never said to kill the man!"

"But that's what a Capital offense means, punishable by death. I have his arrest warrant right here."

"I know what a Capital offense is! But I would remember giving an order like that." Dewar skimmed the document. "Oh, balderdash, I'm using the wrong stamp!"

An assistant entered. "Lord Llewellyn to see you, sir."

Llewellyn entered wearing a stylish black satin corset, with pieces of fish netting draped over his shoulder. Katie Evans stumbled in, shackled to his arm. She accommodated his Lordship's fetish by wearing tattered slave rags and pinning up her long dark hair in a masculine fashion.

"Ah, Larry, how's the party going? Have you got them all warmed up for me?"

"The British are coming!"

"We are the British, you corked port!" The governor wriggled his nose at the odor of booze emanating from the pair. "What? Did you lose the key again? Well, I don't have it. Oh … try the linen closet upstairs." He waved at the girl. "Hello, Katie!"

An extremely drunken Katie snorted, her face turning bright red.

Dewar continued to shout. "Nice to see you!"

"No … King William's forces, they're coming for us!" Llewellyn gasped. "The Euro-strumpets just told me."

"Oh Larry, you've been getting into the absinthe again!"

"Well, of course. Not as much as her tonight, obviously. But this was overheard firsthand from Dr. MacAskill not ten minutes ago."

Dewar's round eyes widened. "British, my booty! It's a bloody Dutch invasion, that's what it is!"

"British, Dutch, what's the difference? They're taking over the city!" Llewellyn hyperventilated, flailing his arms. "Shit! What shall we do?"

"We have a plan," Sleemans interjected coolly.

Dewar stood up. "Bloody traitors! Shit, what'll we do?"

Another assistant knocked on the door. "This just came from Constable Blower."

Dewar's face lit up. "Ah, good old Blower!" He read, not comprehending a single word, before handing the note over to Sleemans. "What does this mean, then?"

Sleemans skimmed over it. "You've been accused of exceeding your authority and charged with high treason. You're to be returned to England immediately, where you'll be hanged before King William."

"Well, that's a bit of rotten luck." Llewellyn's head shook.

"Both of you," Sleemans said.

Llewellyn looked up in disbelief. "Me? But I'm so wealthy!"

"Exceeding my authority? It's not my fault if the bloody pigeons didn't make it back!" Dewar argued. *My God it gets lonely at the top! Everyone wants a bloody piece!*

"The militia will surely be on their way here," Sleemans explained. "We do have a plan."

"We should give ourselves up and blame everything on Cardinal Grimaldi. We'll say he used God's powers to sway us," Llewellyn suggested.

The governor marched back and forth. "That's good. By the time they track him down in Germany, King James should already be back on the throne."

"Yes, well he's *in* it, not on it." Sleemans shook his head and addressed the wall. "It boggles the imagination."

"Are you sure it's a good idea speaking in front of...?" Llewellyn nodded towards Katie.

"It's fine, she's mute. I wish they were all mute!" Dewar paused. "We'll attack the invaders. Send the slaves first!"

"It'll have to be slaves; the militia will side with the Whigs. I'm surprised they haven't shown up already," said Sleemans.

"No military?" Llewellyn bit his lip. "Then we'd better send a lot of slaves. Maybe we should arm them?"

"Armed slaves? Are you mad?" Dewar's eyebrows pointed to the ceiling.

Sleemans clapped loudly. "Not to worry, sir. We planned for this, if you remember?"

"We did?"

"Yes. Operation Fuck Off."

Dewar's face lit up. "Ah yes, good thinking, Sleemans!"

"What's that?" Llewellyn asked.

"Well it's simple, you fuck off." Sleemans pointed to the door.

"What'll we do about you know who?" Llewellyn whispered.

"She fucks off too, just not with us."

Dewar turned to shout at Katie again. "Can you fuck off by yourself, Katie?"

Her eyes narrowed as she rattled the chains.

"Oh, right." Dewar opened his drawer and removed a stiletto. "I'm afraid for the good of society, we have no choice."

"You wouldn't." Llewellyn was ready to weep.

"Of course not. Don't worry, Katie! We're only going to cut off your hand!" Dewar considered the freshly upholstered furniture and Persian rug. "Well, not in here, of course."

Katie looked horrified. "Fuh oo!"

Sleemans sighed and picked the lock with a silver toothpick.

"Don't worry, Katie! We're professionals!"

"And we're insured," Llewellyn added. "You'll make a hundred pieces of eight for that hand."

"For a strumpet's hand? A couple o'bob maybe? Does anyone know how to tie a tourniquet?" Dewar asked.

"Your mental defect hasn't quite been categorized yet." Sleemans continued with the lock and the shackles fell away.

Katie retracted her hand quickly.

Dewar was pleasantly surprised. "Ah, just the thing!"

Katie gave them a disgusted pout and rushed from the room, her middle finger pointing straight up.

"Goodnight, Katie!" Dewar roared. "Oh what's the use? Poor girl can't hear me anyway."

Dr. Marcus MacAskill

One and Thirty

Inside the Swiftsure Tavern, people drank, laughed, smoked, and played cards. Glenda the barmaid, a strikingly robust woman in her mid-thirties, served up wine and ale to sailors, merchants, and tradesmen. "Oi, Nessie! Ales on the speed rail!"

Nessie grabbed a tray and dashed over to the big table.

Coggshall briefly eyed her. He didn't remember hiring her; he usually left that kind of thing up to Glenda. He drank a mouthful of ale and gazed heatedly at the stack of gold bars, doubloons, and silver pieces of eight in the middle of the table. *What a haul!* Coggshall slipped a cigar from his jacket pocket and lit up, puffing heavily.

"Over to Mr. Coggshall. Stick or have it?" Theodore Binge asked, elevating the card deck gracefully. He was a tall slender man with black skin and long, silver-brown hair tied back with a silk ribbon. Binge dressed in an extravagant purple suit and shuffled the cards stylishly, like a true seasoned artisan.

Coggshall slid another gold bar across the table.

"Ah. Have it, it is," Binge said, laying down another card.

Coggshall flushed. *There's no way I can lose!* That's why he kept Binge around. It kept the gambling lively.

"And you, Captain Slazarelli?"

"I feel lucky tonight. Have it!" Slasher Al grinned, sucking in tobacco from his clay pipe, adding more gold to the pile. Lash sat on his shoulder watching intently.

"Aye, yer doing better than me tonight, I'll give you that." Binge turned his head. "And you, Magott?"

"Aye, have it." Magott patted his brow with a new silk handkerchief, and then stuffed it back into his tidy jacket pocket.

"We'll have to cancel." Burghill ran his fingers through his matted hair. "Without new slaves we can't go forward."

"This event is going forward, damn it, regardless! Plenty of those ships brought in by the storm are carrying produce that'll go bad soon. Make them offers, they won't have any choice but to sell cheap. Buy it all up for the fayre!" Coggshall signaled his thug Johnny Shipwash.

Shipwash came forth. "Is that the 'cigars' signal or the 'bathroom' one?"

Coggshall grimaced. *Why the hell'd I hire this one again?* "I want big signs all over town."

"Right, big signs, right."

"This town is going to party if I have to round up every rancid whore and slave in Jamaica to do it!"

"S-sure. That don't go on the sign, do it?" Shipwash cocked his head.

Coggshall pointed at the door.

"Right." The thug left quickly.

"Ya do know he's illiterate?" Burghill sneered.

"Then *you* do the bloody signs. Unless yer illegible too?" Coggshall snarled.

"Stick or have it, Mr. Burghill?" Binge asked.

"Have it." Burghill tossed in three more doubloons.

Binge dealt one last card to Burghill and himself. "Dealer sticks. Last discard, gentlemen."

Each man scrutinized his hand and tossed a card.

"What-cha got, then?" Coggshall gazed around the table.

Each man showed his cards. The top three hands belonged to Slasher Al, Magott, and Binge – all totaling thirty each. Burghill laid down a hand totaling less than twenty.

Coggshall coughed on own cigar smoke, having a hand in the low twenties. He growled at Burghill. *Thought he had the bloody ace!* The two men retreated to the table by the fireplace.

"Thought ya had the one?" Burghill asked.

"Jesus Christ! Yer the fucking bookkeeper!"

"Next hand, One and Thirty?" Binge queried, ready to shuffle for the tie-breaker.

Slasher Al and Magott nodded.

"Nothing too fancy there, Binge!" Coggshall called.

"Whatever you say, Mr. Coggshall. Your bet, Captain Slazerelli."

Al's grin stretched ear to ear, accentuating the scar that ran horizontally across his right cheekbone. He took another gold bar from his pocket.

"Getting too rich for my blood." Binge dangled a gold watch and Al nodded. He set the watch on the table.

Coggshall frowned. "Christ! Where's he getting his wealth from? How much of an incentive did you pay him?"

"I ain't paid him yet!" said Burghill.

Al eyed Magott. "Ya can't match that; show us yer bet."

Magott shrugged, looking over at Coggshall.

Coggshall elbowed Burghill. "Time to bring in the bait."

"Thought we were saving her for later?"

Coggshall peered around suspiciously. "Now's as good a time as any." If the pirate Gator Gar was here, the sacrificial redhead would draw him out.

Burghill waved to his two thugs, and they vanished up the stairs.

"I'll be covering Mr. Magott's bet!"

Al's eyes lit up. "Let's see."

Two thugs dragged a young woman along by the hair, her hands and mouth bound with rope. Atia Crisp trembled and her face flushed with tears.

"Just the way you like them." Burghill raised his mug. "Tenderized."

Al seemed astonished. "Hello again, lovely." He licked his lips as his parrot released a vicious growl.

Capitaine la Roche took a mouthful of ale, tipping his hat to cover his face in shadow. From a dimly lit booth he watched. *What is this?* He tapped his fingers against the mug and gazed at the girl. A lump formed in the back of his throat. The assembly of spectators grunted and cheered. She was pushed out for display. Despite the bruises and rope, her beauty was haunting, hair like flame and eyes like emeralds. His stare shifted to Al. The bastard grinned maliciously, already contemplating which way to cut.

"Show us her bubbies!" a spectator yelled, and everyone cheered.

Binge shuffled the cards, peering up at her sympathetically.

The girl eyed the room, stopping on la Roche. They shared a prolonged stare. His attraction instantaneous, he lost himself heart and soul. *I won't let anything happen to her! Will Theodore back me up after all this time?* Back in the day they'd won many games together and made a lot of gold very quickly. There was only one way to find out if they were still on the same side. La Roche set down his mug and in an act of bravado yelled out, "I am in!" He stepped forward into the light and tipped his hat to look Al in the eye. "Deal me in."

Binge's jaw dropped.

"Well, well, well. See what the gales blew in." Al sneered, taking a shot of rum. "Capitaine le Gator Gar."

La Roche lit a pre-rolled cigarette and approached.

Al motioned him to sit. "I heard you was in town."

"What is your bet?" Binge queried.

La Roche took out a coin bag, withdrew five gold doubloons, and tossed them in the pile.

"Deal him in," Al said.

Binge dealt left to right. After three cards each, they all pondered their hands.

"Time hasn't been good to you, has it, Gator Gar? So where've ya been hiding, eh?"

La Roche mused. "Just as kind to you, *fils de pute*."

"Well, I'm out." Binge threw down his cards, glancing at la Roche briefly.

"That was quick!" Al said.

"Stick or have it?" Binge looked at Al.

"Have it."

Binge turned to Magott. "Stick or have it?"

"Have it."

Then finally to la Roche, "Stick or have it?"

"Have it."

Al snickered. "So, Gator Gar or El Capitaine or whatever you're calling yerself, did the storm bring ya in? Or do you just want to have it off with the redhead?"

La Roche studied his cards. "I'm surprised they let you in here, uh? Class this place had."

"Stick or have it?" Binge asked.

"Have it." Al grinned.

"Stick or have it?" Binge looked to Magott.

"Have it."

La Roche took one more card from Binge.

Big Fred and Dogfish wormed their way closer to Slasher Al.

"I raise." Al's eyebrows pointed up. He withdrew another bar of gold from his jacket.

La Roche glared at the gold. *Merde! Where's he getting his wealth?* To his surprise, le Picard approached with the gold-handled sword.

"Your sword, Capitaine."

La Roche took the weapon smugly and set it on the table. The crowd stirred. "I bet the sword of Don Juan Pérez de Guzmán."

"Henry Morgan gave you that sword." Slasher Al admired the sharp glistening edges and nodded to Binge.

"Yeah, after I won it from him. Get your history straight, uh?"

"Stick or have it?" Binge asked

"Stick," Al replied.

Magott patted his brow with a handkerchief. "Stick."

La Roche tilted his head. "Stick."

"Last discard," Binge called.

Magott threw his cards down and yelled, "out!"

"Bugger!" Coggshall's temple pulsed.

Al laid down his hand, the nine, ten, and jack of clubs.

La Roche laid down the ace, king, and queen of hearts.

"Imagine that!" Binge pointed. "He has the One and Thirty!"

The crowd cheered and groaned in unison, while the girl looked on uncertainly.

"No bloody way!" Al clenched his fist. "Yer a bloody cheat!" Lash tried to flap her clipped wings, but hopped away instead.

"You are free to examine all the cards and my sleeves. I have won fair and square. Not my problem if you're sore about it. She's mine and so is your gold."

Al drew a broad dagger. "Ya bloody cheated, ya'll not be taking her neither!"

Binge and Magott cleared away from the table, while Coggshall and Burghill stood behind the bar.

"Fatima, get over here!" Burghill yelled at his slave, waving his arm. She backed away from the fight.

"Aye, we've lost enough money for one night!" Coggshall added.

Everyone reached for their weapons. La Roche pulled a stiletto from the leather sleeve attached to his belt. He flicked the gold sword to le Picard, who caught it and spun around to defend the flank. Martel was slow on the draw to get his sword, but improvised effectively by kicking a thug in the groin.

"Good timing." La Roche nodded. "You are due for a raise, oui?"

"You should have stayed in your cave, Gator Gar. You ain't getting outta here alive!" Al hissed.

"I should have killed you a long time ago, *connard!*"

The adversaries lunged for each other. Their hats spun to the floor and their blades deflected, lightly grazing each other's flesh. La Roche slipped by his opponent to gain better footing. Al winced as a point pierced his thigh and he fell off balance toppling the table. That's when Dogfish and Big Fred moved in, jabbing swords with le Picard and Martel. A barrage of blades chopped through the air. One cut la Roche's arm. He dropped the stiletto and took out his cutlass. The three Frenchmen arranged themselves in a defensive triangle.

"Ya want her so bad? Ya French swine!" Al staggered, putting all his weight on his good leg. "Kill the bitch!" he yelled at Coggshall.

La Roche turned to her, mortified. *I don't even know your name!* One of the thugs raised a knife to her throat. Time seemed to slow down.

Atia closed her eyes. She was exhausted and in pain. Death didn't seem like such a terrible fate. *I'll see Ma again.* However, the regret of never seeing Livia or the rest of her family confounded her. *Thank you for trying, good sir! My Capitaine!* Atia drew a deep breath and braced herself for the end.

The thug slumped forward. A strong, dark-haired man removed his knife from the back of the villain's head. Streams of blood pooled on the floor. Two more men killed the other thug.

"Ok girl, I got you." The dark-haired man caught Atia just as her legs collapsed beneath her.

"This isn't over. Mark my words!" Al hobbled to the door with Lash on his shoulder. Dogfish helped him along.

A nasty piece of work, him! Atia remembered Al leering at her and Livia. He described in great detail what he had planned for her. She'd never been so grateful to be caged.

"Flog me, uh? You petty thug!" the Capitaine scowled.

Big Fred remained, hovering over him like an impenetrable brick tower. "Come on Frenchie, let's go."

The Capitaine leaned over to pick up his stiletto. Reflexively, he sprang back up, propelling his cutlass through the air, slicing into Big Fred's head. The colossal man toppled to the floor, blood gushing from his skull. Her champion yanked the stained weapon out of the corpse and pointed it at the crowd. "From now on, my protection she is under! You know who I am?" He slipped the stiletto back into its sleeve.

"Um, no," Burghill uttered.

Atia shivered watching the ordeal, and then looked to her other defender.

The striking man with extremely dark rumpled hair gazed at her kindly with warm brown eyes. He returned her to the ground and cut her bonds. "My name's de Kreep. You'll be well, mademoiselle."

She slid her arms around him, kissing his cheek. "Thank you!"

"You've got some nerve, Gator Gar. Get out of my place!" Coggshall sneered.

Atia turned and spat in his direction. "Bloody bastard!"

He rose, ready to throttle her. "Yer as good as dead, little girl!"

The Capitaine stood between them with his cutlass. "She is mine! I will kill anyone who touches her. Anyone!"

"Fine. Keep her the hell outta here! I won't have no thieving pikey in my place anyway!"

The Capitaine pointed his sword at a young African girl. "You there. Pick those up."

Fatima wrapped the coins and the gold bars in the head kerchief that held back her long, dark hair. Placing the winnings in his hat, she handed it over.

"*Merci, jeune dame.*" He stuffed the winnings in his coat and put on the hat.

"*Mon plaisir, monsieur,*" Fatima said.

"Let's go!" The Capitaine clasped Atia's hand. They left through the front entrance, followed by de Kreep and the others. One of the Capitaine's men lingered behind and grabbed a lantern hanging from a metal bracket. He smashed it just outside the door and a fire broke out, barring everyone inside, while they ducked into an alley.

"*Connards!*" Her champion yelled back. "Shitty fucking dive that place turned into!"

"Thank you. Thank you so much!" Atia gasped, hunched over, the pain in her ribs increasing.

"Thank me when we're not in a heap of shit." He lifted one of her arms, while de Kreep took the other and they ran across the street. They passed a wrought iron gate and turned down a path between two properties that led to a sizable yard. Manicured shrubberies and hedges decorated the lawn. Stone pathways lined with exotic flowers led to a pond.

De Kreep gently lowered Atia onto a stone bench and she massaged her side.

"Where do we go, Capitaine?" one man asked.

"I'm thinking! Am I the tour guide?"

De Kreep stroked Atia's hair. "What's your name?"

"Atia, sir. Atia Crisp."

The Capitaine budged in beside her, hastening de Kreep away. "I am pleased to meet you, Mademoiselle Atia, I'm Capitaine Gator Gar. I have won you and you are safely under my protection." He slid his arm around her.

Atia rested her head on his shoulder. He didn't smell entirely unpleasant, a blend of tobacco mixed with ale. She was glad to have a moment of peace. "I don't know how to begin to thank ya." He caressed her back, sending a pleasant chill up her spine. For the first time in days, she felt safe.

"No problem." He kissed her eyebrow. "Let it come naturally, uh? I am curious though, what is your thing? Lick or fuck?"

Atia's jaw dropped. She pulled away, unsure whether she should be angry or amused.

The Capitaine waved his hand. "No, no! You misunderstand. I don't mean *now*."

With her mouth ajar, Atia slapped him hard across the face, wondering if all Frenchmen were this cracked.

He retreated, smirking slightly. "Ah, *le masochisme*! Not my thing."

"Sorry, I don't speak French." She glared at them wearily, crossing her arms over her chest. "Are all o'ya scoundrels then?"

They all shrugged and began to nod.

"Yeah, pretty much." The Capitaine laughed.

A mob with torches approached.

"Everyone get behind the hedge. Keep quiet!" one of the men ordered.

The group ducked, keeping to the shadows. Atia limped away slowly, unconvinced of the Capitaine's usefulness. He followed and took her arm gently. "I did not mean to offend. If it will make you feel better, you can hit the other side so my face looks even." He smiled. "Everything will be fine. Please, come with me." His hand reached for hers.

Atia smiled faintly, scrutinizing his face. His eyes smoldered, breaking down her resistance. *Yer a charming bastard.* A rough exterior perhaps, but handsome by moonlight with an accent that made her heart palpitate. "Where are ya taking me?" Her hand slid into his and they stared at each other, reliving the intensity of their first glance.

Moments passed before la Roche could breathe. Her eyes kept meeting his and her perfect mouth curled into a little smile. Nothing compared to her loveliness. "Someplace safe where you can rest. You seem a little, how you say, worse for wear?"

"Thanks." She sneered, trembling at the night air. "Hurricanes and slavers'll do that."

"I will look after you." He removed his jacket and draped it over her shoulders.

"Where will we go? *La Lune* is not going anywhere," le Picard said.

"Do any of you live here?" Atia asked.

"Cherry Red's, is it still here?" la Roche pondered.

"What? Now?" Le Picard scowled.

De Kreep nodded. "Oui, it is."

"Then we head there."

"Where?" Atia said.

"Cherry Red's. It's a brothel," de Kreep explained.

"Nice place?" Her voice teemed with sarcasm.

"Oui, very nice." He gleamed unabashedly.

"Food, water, shelter is what they have. Let's move out!" La Roche led them along another dark path which came out in an alley riddled with drunkards. They passed a house where a singer and two lute players serenaded a woman in a window with "Man is for the Woman Made". They entered a front yard, pausing beneath the shadows.

"Good luck with that shitty song!" la Roche whispered.

"Might as well be "Troll the Bowel"!" De Kreep said.

A drum beat grew fast and loud through the air. "Here ye, here ye!" the town crier began, "Pirate Gator Gar seen in town! Five hundred pounds for his arrest. Arrest the pirate Gator Gar and his men on sight! Five hundred pounds for his arrest!"

"Safely under your protection, uh?" Le Picard scrutinized Atia, and then the Capitaine. "You go. We'll create a diversion."

"Oui. Cut back across Queens and we will lead them back to Thames," de Kreep added.

Le Picard tapped Martel's shoulder. "We'll lead the rest to High Street, yeah? Then head back to the ship."

"Get her ready to sail as quick as you can," said la Roche. "Leave me if you have to, but protect the ship."

"Oui, Capitaine!"

Le Picard and Martel cut down an alleyway.

"Buccaneers with me!" de Kreep said and shook la Roche's hand. "Always a pleasure, Capitaine. We have to stop meeting like this, people will start to talk."

"*Merci.* You saved our lives back there." La Roche smiled, gripping de Kreep's hand.

Atia lost her balance and was caught by both of them.

De Kreep felt her forehead. "You should get her outta here. She is not well and you have looked better too."

"Thank you." Atia kissed de Kreep on the cheek.

He leaned in to capture her lips before backing away. "That's how you thank me, mademoiselle."

As torchlights and the mob drew closer, the buccaneers snuck away.

"This way, keep your head down." La Roche took Atia's arm. They crossed a misty street near the harbor and slipped along the waterfront. Everything was quiet. The pair reached a black door. Atia leaned against the wall. He knocked twice, then added a third. They waited. He knocked again, but nothing happened.

"Do ya know where we are?" She asked doubtfully.

La Roche pounded the door with his fist. "Ah, she changed the fucking code!"

From inside a voice emerged. "Keep yer pants on, I heard you the first time!" The door opened and high-class strumpet Cherry Banks came into view. She was a lovely woman in her mid-thirties with long mahogany hair covered by a transparent black veil. Her lavish dress was deep purple with a black petticoat and around her neck sat a strand of pearls. Her arms crossed her chest as she stared at them. "Aye, what do ya want?" She glared for a moment and her jaw slacked. "As I live and breathe, Capitaine? I ain't seen you in these parts for years. Why are you knocking on the black door?"

"*Bonjour,* Cherry."

"I didn't recognize you without the beard."

"Oui, a long time it has been."

"Should have shaved it off sooner. I'd have been wet as the moors." Cherry scrutinized Atia. "She'll fetch a pretty penny. A little young for yer taste, ain't she?"

"We need a place to hide." He slid Atia's arm over his shoulder. "Please, *merci.*"

"It's good to see you too." Cherry held the door open and they entered. "What's this all about, then? Who is she?"

"Me name's Atia."

"A pikey eh?"

Atia frowned. "Sorry?"

"A Roman?"

"Aye, my da says we're Romans, descendants of Pikemen."

"Aye, a pikey," Cherry said.

They shuffled down a candlelit corridor lined with fluted fan-shaped brackets made of copper. Stylish fabric lined the walls with a bird and floral motif blended with gold, pink, and blue thread work. A pair of oak Tudor chairs sat at the end of the hall.

"A place to lay low a while, that's all we need," la Roche insisted.

Cherry laughed. "Not by the looks of it!" She glanced down at his bleeding arm.

"Help me get her cleaned up and maybe into new clothes, uh?" He stopped by the kitchen door and grabbed her by the shoulder. "Please, Cherry? For me?"

She smiled. "Anything for you, Capitaine."

The kitchen was less than glamorous. Pots and pans scattered across the counter and moldy bread sat on a wooden board. Dirty plates and cups piled high. "Sorry about the chaos. Housekeeper only comes once a week." Cherry grabbed a glass bottle filled with water and handed it to Atia. "So, where'd ya find her?"

"I took her away from Coggshall and Slasher Al."

Atia slumped on a chair and gratefully guzzled the water. "They still have my sister."

"Sister?" La Roche entertained the notion that he might have two stunning redheads under his protection.

"And you be needing a place to hide?" Cherry eyed Atia. "Don't be drinking so much of that. It's bad for ya."

He grabbed the bottle away. "Where is the clean water?"

"That is the clean water."

La Roche took a mouthful and winced. He took a swig of rum to lose the taste.

"Cleanest I can afford. We're out of the stuff Strangewayes drops off. Right, let's go." She guided them from the kitchen and down the hall, straightening la Roche's collar. "This way, simple scrubber."

"I dunno what that means. Do ya care to repeat it?" Atia challenged.

"She's got fire, she does. Did you swindle her?"

La Roche tipped his hat. "As a matter of fact, I did. Oui."

"Good man! A festering disease Coggshall be!" Cherry opened the door to a well-appointed parlor. In the center of the room, an elegant oak table sat next to a chaise longue bound in a sky-blue brocade with brass fibers. Beneath it, a lush slab of Persian carpet embraced an otherwise plain floor. But the crowning jewel was the whitewashed stone fireplace with a gothic-style mantel.

"Business is good, uh," la Roche said.

"Indeed it is, Capitaine," Cherry boasted. "Maybe I don't have twenty-some-odd girls like Johnny Starr, but this is a first-rate bordello. The place was bustling earlier." She stood at the foot of an ornate staircase. "Lilly! Violante! Come here, quick!" Footsteps thudded against the floorboards. "I'll get Dr. Strangewayes, shall I?" She pulled a handkerchief from her bodice. "Not on the carpet, please."

La Roche wrapped the handkerchief around his wounded arm.

A blonde strumpet galloped down the stairs. She wore a pale pink bodice with matching skirt. She eyed Atia. "She ain't sharing my room. I earned it." She observed la Roche. "Why hello, good sir. What be yer pleasure?"

He tipped his hat. "*Bonjour*, mademoiselle. I have not made your acquaintance."

"They ain't customers, Lilly. They're hurt."

"Oh. Nice to meet you anyway, sir."

"Go heat up the pots and fix this one a bath." Cherry pointed at Atia.

"Aye." Lilly nodded and ran towards the kitchen.

"A pleasure, mademoiselle," la Roche called after her.

"Vie!" Cherry bellowed.

Another stunning strumpet entered the room wearing a black, low-cut witch dress complete with broomstick. It accentuated her voluptuous figure and protruding nipples. She too examined Atia. "Good lips for polishing."

"Polishing?" Atia's eyes narrowed.

"Go fetch Dr. Strangewayes, will you? It's urgent."

"Pleased to meet you, mademoiselle." La Roche tipped his hat, ogling her curves.

"I be late already, but I'll let him know on the way." Vie adjusted the pointy black hat that matched her long dark hair.

"Mum's the word, Vie," Cherry insisted.

"I'll fly." She winked at la Roche before going to the front door.

"Cardinal Grimaldi has a weakness for witches. He leaves for Germany tomorrow, so she wanted to surprise him." Cherry patted his back.

"She can ride my broomstick."

"You've been at sea too long, haven't you, my dear?"

"Hmm, three long days," la Roche lamented.

"Come with me, darling and we'll get you cleaned up." Cherry motioned to Atia. "Care to join us, Capitaine? Or are you going to wait down here?"

"It is tempting, but I think I will bleed down here in case the doctor arrives."

The two women climbed the staircase and la Roche sat down on the chaise longue, stretching out his legs. *So many beautiful women, I hope there's enough blood left tomorrow for my prick to work!*

Theodore Binge

Laudanum and Hallucinations

In his study, Dr. Strangewayes sat in an easy chair beside the window, writing notes in a leather-bound book. For a moment he looked up to see the silhouette of a witch on a broomstick glide by. His eyes opened widely and he continued note-taking. "Long term use of laudanum leads to hallucinations." He put down the quill and massaged his eyes. "Time for sleep, old chum." He set the book aside. "Come along, Boots." A large marmalade cat napped, sprawled out across the width of the desk. "Oh, never mind."

From the back door came three knocks. *Oh, shit*. The doctor reluctantly headed downstairs. After monitoring the events outside when mobs roamed the streets with torches, he feared he'd meet his end with a pitchfork. He passed by the examination room and down the hall to the back. He held up an oil lamp and opened the door cautiously.

The doctor paused for a moment, stretching for the appropriate words. "Well, I must say, this is a switch, you knocking on my door for a change."

Vie stood there boldly, broomstick in hand.

"Are you quite well?" His gaze stumbled onto her pointy hat and costume. "My dear girl, if you get caught dressed like that, the best solicitor in the world couldn't get you off."

"You don't know how right you are, Doctor." She adjusted her hat. "Cherry needs you. People are hurt. One's been cut and he's bleeding pretty good. The other's a girl. She looks like she's been through a hurricane."

"Well, we did just have one." The doctor smiled. "You'd better come inside whilst I get my things."

"Thanks Doc, but I must fly. Just passing on the message is all." Vie turned and slipped into the blackness of the back yard.

"Lucky broom." Strangewayes closed the door to grab his medical bag and changed his clothes.

Down near the waterfront at the Crooked Compass, drunken patrons broke into a chorus of "Once, Twice, Thrice". Upstairs in Burghill's sitting room, Slasher Al lay sprawled on a plush sofa, his injured leg propped up beneath a mound of pillows. Tending to him was Dr. MacAskill, who tied a loop and finished stitching the gashed leg.

"No, stop! Yer killing me!" Al protested.

The doctor's eyes narrowed. "Oh, ya big baby. I've seen bigger wounds than this at a Bris!"

"I'm so tired; he must have got the artery."

"If he had, you'd be dead by now. But ya lost a shit load of blood, so shut the fuck up!" The doctor instructed with all the concern of a galliwasp munching on its prey. He'd seen enough carnage from this maniac.

"Jesus!" Al sneered, clutching the edge of the sofa.

"I don't cure lepers." MacAskill finished the bandage. "You'll need to stay off it for a while."

"How am I supposed to get around then?"

"I don't know. What am I, yer fuck'n mother? Try riding a wheelbarrow for Christ's sake!" *I could get away with it,* MacAskill thought. *I could say he bled out.*

"Can ya give me something for pain at least? Laudanum?"

"That shit leads to hallucinations." The doctor grabbed a bottle of rum. "Here, take two of these and fuck off!" He rummaged through his medical bag. There sat a bottle of laudanum and a bottle of poison in a small vial. He eyed Al again. *Time to do the world a public service - ya sick bastard!*

To the doctor's dismay, Pikestaff with Gibbet on his shoulder entered with Jag'd Jayne and Mike, another of Art's thugs. They immediately paused at the bar to fetch a drink.

Fuck'n hell! Another missed opportunity! MacAskill snapped his bag shut. "I thought you were supposed to guard Coggshall?"

"He had me guarding the other pikey." Pikestaff stuffed tobacco into his pipe and struck a match. "Just who is this Frenchman anyway?"

"Gator Gar it was!" Al hissed. "I'll have his liver for this!"

"And you're certain it was him?" MacAskill stared at Al doubtfully.

"Who?" Jayne interjected.

"A pirate who used to serve under Henry Morgan. A Frenchman," Mike said.

Jayne grabbed a rum shot. "With all the buzz, I thought it be someone important."

Al took a swig of rum. "Gator Gar is in town. Believe me that is important. There be a lotta pirates who'd like to have a chat with him."

"Jesus Christ on sweaty Palm Sunday, not one of ya's got the brains to find the chamber pot under yer arse! We got bigger problems than Gator Gar. No one's seen him in nearly four years. Those are King William's forces out there." MacAskill pointed.

"Whoever he was, he ain't worth causing a panic." Jayne poured another shot.

"Was? Careful, laddie, Gator Gar's killing total is higher than you can count up to. If it is him, he's not to be messed with." MacAskill turned to Pikestaff. "What the hell were you thinking sending mobs into the streets without checking with us first?"

"Mr. Coggshall wants 'em found." Pikestaff puffed his pipe.

"Mr. Coggshall wants 'em found." MacAskill imitated and cleared his throat. "Ya work for Bleedin Art, not fuck'n Coggshall. And don't ya forget it, unless ya want to find yerself on a slave galley bound for the Barbary Coast!"

"Look what he done to me!" Al snapped, finding some solace in the rum. "There's a bounty on him and I'm the one collecting! Coggshall is personally granting a Letter of Reprisal on account of me attack. I won't be denied what's due me! I want his liver!"

"Or I could open this back up and let some air in," MacAskill offered, wrenching Al's leg, causing him to scream. "If Gator Gar is here, we'll find him. Quick and quiet before the Whigs do."

"Aye, sir, we'll find 'em," Pikestaff assured. "Quick and quiet."

Inside Cherry's posh bedroom, Lilly dumped a large kettle of hot water into a copper bathing tub and lit the wall-mounted oil lamps. Steam rose and the entire room transformed into a sensual sanctuary. Silk flowers sat in crystal vases and luscious velvet curtains hung from a brass rail over the window, matching the drapes of the canopy bed.

Atia felt dazed by the grandeur. She was steered towards a large oak wardrobe, where dozens of dresses, skirts, petticoats, overcoats, bodices, and corsets all hung from wooden hooks.

Cherry patted her shoulder. "You'll be needing to get changed. Take a gander, see if any of them tickle yer fancy. The Capitaine's buying." She checked the progress of the bath. "That's almost got it. Just needs some of this." Cherry sprinkled scented flower petals into the water and leaned in close to Lilly. "I admit it's a shock to see him."

"He's the Frenchman ya told me about?" Lilly asked.

"The very one."

"Kinda old, ain't he?"

"It ain't the age; it's the size that counts! And Lilly dear, he counts."

Atia draped a couple of choices over a chair. First, a nightdress of creamy satin, sleeveless with thin shoulder straps accompanied by a regal blue robe. The other was a deep forest green bodice with gold beading and a matching petticoat.

Cherry rested her hands on the edge of the tub and eyed Atia. "And her, she's a double for Jacquotte. Just his type."

"I have to go. I must find me sister." Atia trembled, and her limbs felt like they were trudging through cold wet sand.

"The Capitaine will find your sister. We need to get ya cleaned up." Cherry waved her over. "Well, get undressed, girl. I can help wash yer hair if you like."

Lilly left the room to refill the kettle while Atia approached the tub shuddering fiercely. She tried to unlace her dress, but her fingers lost their strength.

"Let me help you, you're shaking like a leaf."

Atia nodded.

Cherry assisted and Atia soon sunk into the hot water.

"Vie's just gone to get the doctor for you, so you just relax now." Cherry brought out a tin cup and a bar of soap. She saturated Atia's long red hair before working the bar gently through. "Well, yer too civil to be one of his usual picks. 'Course I haven't seen him for years. He is a bit more seasoned than I remember."

"That smells pretty." Atia closed her eyes, drinking in the sweet flowery air. It reminded her of the small wildflower garden her ma kept when they lived in Hope Bay.

"Thank Dr. Strangewayes when you see him. He makes special soaps with honey and herbs. Clever man, he is."

Atia massaged some on her face and all over her body, washing away the filth of the past few days. "I think met him. Seems nice, he does."

"He is that. When did you meet him?"

Atia splashed water on her face and remembered hanging onto the rail of the *Aeolus*. A strange tingling started at the base of her neck and made her head throb. "When we was…" her eyes enlarged. "We was caged." She gasped for air – her lungs felt as though they were closing. "Livia? Where's Livia?" Her eyes rolled to the back of her head and everything went black.

Cherry pulled Atia's head from the water. She lightly slapped the girl's face with no response and brushed a strand of hair from her eyes. *Bloody hell! He's been away for four years without a word, and then brings back a stray that faints!* "Are ya okay?" Cherry smacked Atia's face again. "Hello in there? Shit! Help! Capitaine! Lilly!"

Seconds later, footsteps could be heard on the staircase and in the hall. Both the Capitaine and Lilly burst into the room.

"What is wrong?" He stared down at the water.

"She passed out, said something about a cage, and then fainted. Help me lift her out."

The Capitaine rushed to Atia's side to help lift her body from the water.

"She don't look so good," Lilly said.

"Thanks genius, give us a hand!" Cherry snapped, grabbing Atia's legs. All three carried her from the tub to the canopy bed.

The Capitaine propped Atia's head against a pillow and stared longingly at her bare body.

Cherry shook her head. "She's just your type, too."

"Redhead?" He grinned.

"No, unconscious and naked."

The Capitaine smirked. "That was one time! I didn't know she'd been drinking wormwood wine. I thought she was a virgin!"

Cherry batted her eyes. "A virgin in these parts? A likely story, you scoundrel."

"Just because I was conscious doesn't mean I was any less drunk than she was."

"I don't want to know." Lilly shook her head, handing him a blanket.

A knock came at the door and Dr. Strangewayes materialized. "Don't mind me, I'm just playing follow the blood."

"Evening, Doctor. Thanks for coming so late." Cherry took his hand warmly.

"Well, you know what the Christians say about the wicked? I hope you don't mind, but I let myself in. Vie had to fly."

"Not at all. We got wounded and fainted here."

"I see that." The doctor did a double take when he beheld the Capitaine. "Oh, good God!"

"No see, long time, uh?"

"I heard you were back. Hence the mobs in the streets." Strangewayes leaned over Atia, opening each of her eyelids. "And she only just fainted?"

"Just now in the bath," Cherry said.

The doctor felt Atia's pulse before examining her neck and chin. "Hmm, delayed shock."

"Will she be well again?" The Capitaine stroked her hair.

"Yes, I should think so. Her color's good aside from the bruising. Probably hasn't eaten in a long time, poor girl. She's been through a terrible lot. Has she been drinking water?"

"She drank a lot when she got here. Not the clean stuff, though. We're all out of that." Cherry leaned against the bedpost.

"I'll have more delivered in the morrow. I don't want her getting dehydrated. For now, just keep her warm. Now, let's see that arm." The doctor cut away the bloodied fabric of the sleeve. A large curved gash ran from bicep to his forearm. "Well, sorry if I seemed startled, Capitaine. It is good to see you again. What winds blew you back in? Was it a hurricane, by chance?"

"Oui. Not my choice."

"We're going to need more hot water and plenty of booze for disinfection."

"Right-o." Lilly ran out the door.

"I could go for a good disinfecting right now." The Capitaine winced. "Whatever that means."

"You're lucky. It's only a flesh wound, but I'm still going to have to clean it before stitching it."

"It's clean enough, just stitch it."

"Oh, don't be a baby." The doctor took gauze and a meager supply of alcohol from his bag. "Where did you find her?"

"She wandered in one day, looking for food and a place to sleep," Cherry began.

"Not Lilly, Sleeping Beauty here." He motioned to Atia and dabbed the wound.

"*Merde*! Funny story. I won her in a card game from Coggshall and Slasher Al."

"Well done, old chum!"

The Capitaine stroked Atia's hair. "Beautiful, she is. A certain look there is in her eyes. Now she is mine."

Cherry crossed her arms over her chest. "Careful, Capitaine. Your heart's throbbing worse than yer cock!"

Strangewayes put down the gauze and readied a needle and thread.

Lilly arrived with hot water and a new bottle of alcohol.

"Good timing. We're both going to need some for this part." The doctor smiled.

"Will Russian vodka do?" Lilly asked.

"Oui, nicely, it will." The Capitaine eagerly uncorked it with his teeth to take a mouthful.

"Did she say her name at all?" Strangewayes grabbed the bottle and splashed some on the wound.

"*Putain*! Her name is Atia."

"Ah yes, that would be Atia Crisp."

"Familiar with Coggshall's girls, you are, Sander?"

Strangewayes's eyebrows peaked. "My goodness, no. You're completely wrong. This girl is not one of Coggshall's." He took a swig of vodka and handed it to Cherry. "Why, she's a shipwreck survivor. I saw her earlier today with her sister."

The Capitaine's mouth dropped. "Folly Bay is where she was found?"

"Yes, the ship broke up there. She and her sister may be the only survivors, if Livia is still alive." Strangewayes held a lantern over Atia to reveal the bruises on her face.

"I saw that ship, but nothing I could do; straight into Folly Bay they were headed." The Capitaine lifted the blanket to inspect the heavy bruising to her arms and ribs.

"You didn't notice those?"

"I hadn't got around to undressing her yet. But it's normal for around here, no?" The Capitaine shrugged, replacing the blanket. "I thought she was a prostitute. I feel kinda bad."

Cherry took a swig of vodka. "How did Coggshall get her?"

"Thank Magott and the sheriff." The doctor began to stitch up the arm.

"Who's Magott?" the Capitaine asked.

"A local sugar farmer and slave trader. He sold them to Coggshall and our town sheriff declared it legal."

Cherry shook her head. "If they're indentured, then it was legal. Poor girl, her sister be as good as dead."

"She's right. Slasher Al always cuts up one of Coggshall's girls whenever he's in town. It's his way of protecting his investments, offering up a lamb for slaughter." Lilly sucked back some vodka.

"Strange as it may seem, Atia's the lucky one. I myself would be willing to pay handsomely if anyone could find her sister, before it's too late," the doctor said.

"I think we can find her for ya, Doc. We could ask Edmund; he's a stand-up gentleman. He ain't like his father at all," Lilly insisted.

Strangewayes appeared horrified at the prospect.

"She's right. He's different; one of them scholarly types. He's always a gentleman to the ladies and I know you won't believe me, Doc, but he don't mistreat slaves either," Cherry said.

"He's probably the best chance we got to finding her. If I hurry, I might catch him before he locks up," said Lilly.

"Well then, I think it's a superb idea. What do I know?"

"Go on, then. But don't say anything to anyone about the Capitaine or his pikey, right? Not a word." Cherry pointed her finger at Lilly.

"Lilly, if by some chance you're able to find her, send word to me straight away at the apothecary. If I'm not there, inform Mrs. Beazley. She'll know what to do."

"Aye, Doc." Lilly smiled and departed.

"She's a good girl," the Capitaine said.

"Yes. Her heart's in the right place," the doctor agreed.

"All me girls are good people. I don't want nothing to happen to them." Cherry eyed the doctor. "We should tell him."

"Moi? Tell me what?" The Capitaine blinked slowly, clearly drunk.

"The real reason Al is here is to kill me and my girls."

"A mutual friend informed us. Coggshall plans to kill all of Cherry's girls and replace them with his own," the doctor said.

"It's his way of competing with Johnny Starr's brothel and we're not waiting for them to come to us," Cherry added.

"Coggshall and his men are all thugs and creeps," the Capitaine deduced.

"Indeed," the doctor agreed. "They now run the city."

"No kidding? Those knuckleheads? This place has gone to shit."

"Well, to put it frankly, you lot all died off, whilst the wolves were left behind to guard the sheep." Strangewayes finished the last stitch on the wound and sprinkled it with sulfur.

"What a day this turned out to be. What are you planning to do?" the Capitaine slurred.

"We're going to *do* Coggshall and Burghill too. He's the one who cut Katie's tongue out. Magott, Bleedin Art and Pikestaff."

"You were going to take them on by yourselves? They may be stupid thugs, but there are many of them, professional killers. We'd better kill them all, right down to the last one. Including Art and his men. We should attack by force right away. My buccaneer friend is in town. I could find him and we can teach these thugs a lesson." The Capitaine collapsed beside Atia.

"We? You haven't lost a thing, Capitaine." Cherry felt a flicker of adoration. "However, ya ain't going anywhere tonight in the state you're in. We'll talk about this in the morrow."

"Yes, Capitaine. You must rest now, and I must prepare the apothecary." The doctor packed up his medical bag.

"What do I do with them?" Cherry peered over at the Capitaine. He stroked Atia's hair, doting over her like a pet.

"Make him drink clean water, lots of it. Let her sleep as much as she needs. Give her water and food when she wakes up. Someone should stay with her; she shouldn't be left alone."

The Capitaine put his hand in the air. "I will care for her."

"When she wakes up, she will be in a lot of pain." Strangewayes set a small bottle of laudanum on the bed table. "Do you remember that stuff, Capitaine?"

"Ha!" He face flushed red. "Not really, no. Well, yes. Don't you have any opium tablets?"

"This should be more effective for her type of injuries; no doubt more will manifest. Only a few drops."

"Thank you, Doctor, I remember. She will be fine. *Merci, my friend.*"

They shook hands.

"At least Atia has landed someplace safe, for now."

Cherry escorted the doctor out, glancing back at the fugitives in her bed. Jealousy raged within her, especially when he caressed Atia's face and uttered, "I will look after you, *ma chérie.*" *Not a bloody word for four years! Not even a note!* Once downstairs, she stomped her feet. "Bloody hell! This changes everything! Ya know what they'll do to us when they find out he was here?"

"Please take a deep breath," Strangewayes soothed, massaging her arms. "On the contrary, somebody had to make the first move."

"Right, well, whoever makes the first move is usually the first casualty!"

"That's not always the case." He cradled her hands. "Our next steps are critical. The hurricane bringing buccaneers here may have tipped the scales back in our favor. Don't give up hope, especially now that help has finally arrived."

A thin layer of sea mist covered Thames Street. Members of the mob disbanded, leaving only a few men standing guard with torches. Le Picard and Martel raced along, keeping to the shadows. The north dock soon came into view.

La Lune's crew busily prepared for departure. Harbormaster Pepys argued with Delacroix, while Major Paine observed from behind.

"French shipmaster, you must leave straight on. Make way!" Pepys said.

"Oui, we are leaving," Delacroix called back, "but we must wait for our Capitaine!"

Le Picard and Martel arrived but were blocked by Constable Blower and two city guards who came storming from the King's Ground and onto the long arm of the north dock.

Le Picard held his breath while he ensured the handle of the gold sword was hidden beneath his coat.

"They might mistake you for your brother," Martel said.

"I don't want my relation to be a problem, you be the Capitaine." He pushed Martel in front of him.

"Me?" Martel pointed to himself.

Constable Blower charged towards *La Lune*. "I want that ship stopped. Search every crack in her stinking French hull!"

"I already did that." Pepys turned to Blower. "This ship's been ordered to leave."

"On whose authority?"

"On my authority, if ya please," Major Paine spoke sharply.

"A wanted pirate was seen in the city," Blower huffed. "The Frenchman Gator Gar."

"Gator Gar? Ya don't say. Well, ya won't find him on that ship." Pepys lit his pipe. "I searched that ship meself. She's loaded to the gills with sugar and carrying minimal weapons."

Paine lit his cigar. "Don't sound like your man."

"They paid their fee in gold dust from a locked chest," Pepys said.

"Then it's a merchant vessel," Paine explained. "Regardless, we want a peaceful transition and all ships are allowed to leave, pirate or not."

Blower snorted with irritation. "Where's her captain?"

Le Picard nudged Martel in front of him and hid his own face behind the rim of his hat. *Just don't mess this up!*

"I am Capitaine of this ship," Martel declared.

"Aye, you're free to go, Captain."

"Oui, *merci*." Martel swiftly led them forward along the gangway. "*Au revoir*."

Le Picard patted his brow once they reached the deck. *How the hell did we get by again? Surely Major Paine is more diligent than this?*

"Thank God, you are back!" Delacroix exhaled deeply. "Where's the Capitaine?"

"Let her go, fore and aft!" le Picard ordered.

"Long boats away! Prepare to make sail!" Martel shouted authoritatively, and then bumped into a crewman on his way up to the quarterdeck.

"*Mon dieu*." Le Picard shook his head while the men scrambled to get the ship mobile. "The Capitaine is not coming. Prepare for departure."

"We can't leave without the Capitaine!" Delacroix looked shocked.

"That is an order, Delacroix!" Le Picard gazed back at Port Royal. *I told you it wasn't a good idea, Capitaine!*

To be continued…

Laudanum and Hallucinations

About the Authors

MJL EVANS always wanted to be a writer since she was ten years old. Her motto - it's never too late in life to get your act together and do something you really love. No Quarter: Dominium is her first book series. Her sense of humor has been shaped by BBC comedies, while her dramatic side has been influenced by independent/foreign movies. She looks forward to starting the series No Quarter: Wenches.

You can connect with MJL Evans on Twitter at
@artistmjlevans or **noquarterseries@gmail.com**

GM O'CONNOR is a huge movie fan, writer and visual artist. A lover of sci-fi and history, half his brain lives in the 17th century while the other half sails perpetually through space. He hopes to one day bring the No Quarter Series to film and/or graphic novel format.

You can connect with GM O'Connor on Twitter at
@gm_oconnor or **noquarterseries@gmail.com**

Please visit our website or Facebook page to be the first to know when the adventure continues…
http://noquarterseries.com/
https://www.facebook.com/noquarterseries/
If you enjoyed our story we would love it if you could please write us a review!

No Quarter: Dominium – The Complete Series
Now available!

www.ingramcontent.com/pod-product-compliance
Lightning Source LLC
Chambersburg PA
CBHW020311150626
46552CB00022B/2762

* 9 7 8 0 9 9 4 8 7 4 4 0 5 *